Folks You Meet in

Longs®

and other stories

Lee Cataluna

ISBN 0-910043-71-X

This is issue #86 (Fall 2004) of *Bamboo Ridge, Journal of Hawai'i Literature and Arts* (ISSN 0733-0308).

Published by Bamboo Ridge Press
Printed in the United States of America
Indexed in the American Humanities Index
Bamboo Ridge Press is a member of the Council of Literary Magazines and Presses (CLMP).

Cover and title page: *Longs Drugs downtown: Hotel/Bishop, circa late 1960s,* by Doug Young
Use of Longs trademark courtesy of Longs Drugs Stores
Section break photographs: *Longs Drugs: A Tradition of Caring 1938–1988,* copyright © 1988 Longs Drugs Stores.
Typesetting and design: Wayne Kawamoto

Bamboo Ridge Press is a nonprofit, tax-exempt corporation formed in 1978 to foster the appreciation, understanding, and creation of literary, visual, or performing arts by, for, or about Hawai'i's people. This project was supported in part by grants from the National Endowment for the Arts (NEA) and the State Foundation on Culture and the Arts (SFCA), celebrating over thirty years of culture and the arts in Hawai'i. The SFCA is funded by appropriations from the Hawai'i State Legislature and by grants from the NEA.

NATIONAL
ENDOWMENT
FOR THE ARTS

Bamboo Ridge is published twice a year. For subscription information, back issues, or a catalog, please contact:

Bamboo Ridge Press
P.O. Box 61781
Honolulu, HI 96839-1781
(808) 626-1481
brinfo@bambooridge.com
www.bambooridge.com

5 4 3 2   05 06 07 08 09

CONTENTS

I.
FOLKS YOU MEET IN LONGS

II.
BABES, WHY YOU ACKING LI'DAT FOR?

III.
BACK TO SCHOOL

IV.
VALUE BOOK

V.
MR. AND MRS. LONGS

ACKNOWLEDGMENTS

To Gerald Saito and all of Longs for being so cool.

To Keith Kashiwada for invaluable input, insight, and inspiration.

To Kumu Kahua Theatre, a most fertile garden where writers can grow.

To the original cast, designers, and crew of the stage play Folks You Meet in Longs.

To Curtis Lum, who let me steal his story.

DEDICATION

To Jim, who would go to Longs for me if I was too sick to go myself.

INTRODUCTION

People have suggested that these stories could happen in numerous other places: little neighborhood grocery stores, on TheBus, at beloved plate lunch counters. Some have been quite insistent on this point and offer up their "Folks You Meet in . . . " stories from other locations.

But to me, Longs is unique. It is the place you go to when you're in pain. The aisles serve as passageways through the various stages of life. It is the place young girls go to furtively buy the items that mark their transition into womanhood. It is the place old folks find the salves for wounds acquired over the miles. When a woman is pregnant, she's in Longs almost as often as she's in the ladies' room.

It is the ever-ready storehouse to visit when you need a last-minute birthday card, when you're putting together a local-style CARE package for a college student on the Mainland, or when you've left home in a hurry without provisions and need a toothbrush and socks.

Longs is where people go to when they NEED. On the shelves, you find relief, distraction, healing; and if there's no product for what ails you, there's often a kind clerk, an intuitive fellow-shopper, or a bit of overheard conversation that is enough to keep you going.

And yes, many of these pieces were heard in those hallowed aisles.

I.

FOLKS YOU MEET IN LONGS

NADINE TAM SING

–

LONGS WORKER

YOU KNOW HOW WHEN YOU WATCH MOVIES, THEY ALWAYS have the bartender guy who seen it all? Let me tell you, bartender man neva seen nothing. I worked here twenty years already. I seen it all. I seen it all two, three times. The whole world comes into Longs.

I see the ones that come in all sick when they should be home in bed. Some of them, they too proud to have somebody help them. They young and strong and cannot believe they have to take pills. They should be lying on the couch, taking a nap, watching TV, but they come here, drag themselves through the store, pick up their pills, and go back to work. Some of them, they just don't have nobody. Nobody to pick up their medicine for them. They should be at home, but they don't have choice.

I see the fat-a-boolas who come in and spend fifty dollars on couple cases Slim Fast Shakes. Two weeks later, they back in, spending more money on DexaTrim and Korean Diet Tea and sugar-free gum. I take notice when they lose couple pounds. I watch when everything they lost they find again. They come in and buy Milk Duds and Cheetos and Oreos Double Stuff. I don't say nothing. I just ring 'em up, bag 'em up, count off their change. I see the eyes, though. All shame.

I see plenty of that. Shame eyes. Eighth grade girls buying pads. High school boys buying rubbers. Old men buying diapers. I see the young girls trying to hide the at-home tests in the bottom of their basket. I don't say nothing.

Most people, they come in and buy their hope. They hope they going lose weight or look younger or not hurt so much all the time. They hope this eye shadow going impress Leighton Pacheco or that Ace bandage going fix their leg.

Sometimes it works. The skin clears up or the pain goes away or the hair dye looks good. Then they're back. Then they're regulars, they hooked, and hoo! they get mad when something happens in the stockroom and we don't have their stuff on the shelves. They think it's against them, like we the ones standing in their way, keeping their stuff away from them on purpose. Like we in it to make them suffer.

I see the grampas coming in wearing their grandkids black rock and roll T-shirts. I see kids coming in wearing their grampa's soft, buss-up cotton undershirts with so much yellow stains look like one pattern. I see the tourist girls coming in wearing sand on their feet and not too much else.

Sometimes they take stuff, and I see that too. I don't say nothing. If you gotta steal from Longs, you get problems in your life that nothing on these shelves gonna solve.

People don't realize that they walk around with their needs on their face like a grocery list pinned to their shirt. I need attention, I need distraction, I need help. I seen it. I seen it every day. If that movie bartender came in, I could take one look at his eyes and tell him which aisle he was going first, and he would be surprised. Nine-B half-way down, third shelf. And sir, next week, going on sale. Twenty years. I seen it all.

MRS. TAKENAKA

–

WEDNESDAY MORNING REGULAR

YOU HEARD ABOUT HARRIET?
Ai-ya, you neva hear about Harriet?
She stay hospital. You neva hear?
She hit her head. Terrible, you know. She stay wit one coma. Or maybe so not one coma, maybe was concussion.
Wait now. Was coma or was concussion?
Something like that. I remember so, start with one 'c.'

Anyways, she was at the daughter's house cuz the daughter just had the baby, yeah?
You neva know the daughter was going have one baby?
Third one already. So cute. From that good looking Filipino boy.
The first two not from him, but. They not so cute.

So Harriet went the daughter's house. She live behind the old Emjay's, you remember over there?
So Harriet was inside the bathroom and the daughter just had put one new bathmat down, you know, in the place in between the toilet and the edge of the shower.
Not the kind with the rubber underneath kind.
The kind he more like terry-cloth kind. Slippery, that's why I no buy that kind. And more expensive.
Harriet wen stand up from the toilet and she was reaching down for pull up her pantyhose, and her jade ring had catch on the expensive bathmat, and she was pulling and pulling because I guess so the prong part was stuck, yeah?

You seen how big that ring? That's the kind they used to call cocktail ring, but Harriet, she always get that on, even when she only going shopping.

So she was pulling and pulling and somehow that bathmat went up and Harriet went down and when the daughter found her six hours later, she was flat on the bathroom floor, all blue.
Her head crack the toilet bowl open just like one egg and all the water came out.
They thought she wasn't breathing but the blue was from the toilet water, you know how they get that blue toilet water thing to clean? So Harriet was blue, tankobu on her head, pantyhose all wrap around her ankles.
Terrible, yeah?

So she went hospital.
I cannot remember if was coma or concussion. Something with one 'c.'
Three days already.
She still yet all blue.

The thing get hard time to come off.

Ai-ya, you don't know Harriet? I think so she moved 'Aiea before you came, yeah?

Ah, poor thing. Nice lady, you know. Always with the big jade ring.
Except not now in the hospital.
They had to cut that thing off.
Now she only get the blue.

CORINNA MOLINA
–
JANESSA'S FRIEND

AY, JANESSA, TRY LOOK DA PURPLE NAIL POLISH. YOU
should get 'em.
Match with your hickey necklace.
No act like you can hide 'em with makeup. I can see the thing shining
through like purple panties underneath white shorts. Shoot, not too
obvious you wearing turtleneck to school for three days, kudeesh.

Here, get the purple nail polish with the sparkle stuff inside and then get
the spray-on body glitter for your neck for da night time look. Get the
plum passion lipstick so you can leave all kind marks on him and no even
gotta suck.
Rub 'em all on top his shirt so when his mother wash clothes she think her
son was bleeding.

Oh, you gotta check out this lotion.
Look the lotion, Janessa.
You should get the lotion.
You no like chap.
You chap? You chapping? You chap planny, no, you?
You such a chappa', Janessa.

Look the small cute little perfume get.
So cute, yeah?
You should get that, Janessa. You should get perfume.
You should get deodorant.
Get the all-over kind, you know. You should get the all-over kind.

All over, you know.
You should buy couple.
Buy the shelf.

You know, if you put planny eyeliner, going draw the attention to your face
so people not going be staring at the muffler burns all on your neck.
Get the black eyeliner.
Not brown-black.
No, that's just black. Get the black-black kind.
That's the kind.
Draw attention to your eyes, that's why. You no like people staring at your
neck cuz look kinda buss.

Or just buy the thick-kind scar-kind pack-'em-on makeup.
Put like Bondo on top your neck.
Make everybody think you hiding one zipper for keep your head on like
the Frankenstein lady.

I no think so this even your aisle, Janessa. Come, we go find your aisle.
The one close to the pharmacy.
The one with all your stuffs that you need.
Maybe get some hickey cream right next to all the other stuffs.
Maybe get cream you can rub on top your neck for take 'em off so you no
gotta sleep your aunty's house one more night.
I promise, Janessa, look so obvious.

DEATRA LANNING
–
BRANDON'S MOMMY

BRANDON, COME HERE.
Brandon, come here.
Brandon.
Brandon.
Brandon. Come over here Mommy said.
Put that down and come over—
Brandon, don't you get that look on your face Brandon. I better not see that look on your—

There's the look. What I said? What Mommy said, Brandon?

I told you don't you give me no look and then you give me the look and—

Oh! Don't you turn your back on Mommy, Brandon! Don't you dare turn your back on Mommy or you're gonna get it. I didn't go through nine months hard labor pop my belly button ring, stretch marks starting from my neck for this, Brandon.

Brandon come here.
You come here, Brandon.

Ay, God, don't you run away, Brandon! Don't you run—

Damn kid, come back here. You young and you fast but Mommy get the car keys and the money for McDonald's so you ain't getting very far without me. Come back here. Brandon! Don't you go up those stairs. Don't go up the—

Oh so what. Mommy going take the escalator two steps at a time and I going reach the top first. I going get you, you little brat. Six years old and running around. You just like yo' father.

Brandon, I going leave you in the shopping mall, Brandon. That's it. I'm going. I'm leaving you all by yourself in the shopping mall, Brandon. I going. Mommy going. You not going have no Mommy no more. How you like that?!

Brandon! Come back here!

TOMMY PINTO

—

LIVES AT HOME

MY MOTHER CALL ME ON MY CELL: "BOY!" SHE TELL ME, "I need coffee filters! You gotta get me coffee filters!" Shoot, I tell her. I go Longs after work. "Not after work!" she tell me, "Right now!" What, coffee emergency? "No ask questions! Just get 'em NOW!"

She no tell me what kind. She no tell me how big. All she like is coffee filters and as much as I can find. I get her one box with 60 inside. She send me out for more. I get her one box with 120 inside. She send me out for MORE. I go four different Longses, buy out every store. She like more. What the hell you doing, Ma? She tell me 'as one project for my small nephew's church class. They making Virgin Mary procession like it's one Aloha Week float and she need the coffee filters for make the ruffly-part of the kāhilis. Ho Ma, I tell her. So authentic. Shut up, she tell me. And if get any more coffee filters out there that you left behind in Longs, you better hope I don't find out about it 'cause you going get it!

They up all night. I try go sleep in the parlor but they wake me up so I can help stuff coffee filters in the chicken wire on top the broomstick. Afterwards, we gotta go outside in the backyard to spray paint 'em all the different colors for the islands. I tell her I didn't know Virgin Mary worked Hawaii Visitors Bureau. She tell me no talk like that, so blasphemous.

The next morning, I all tired, but my small nephew look so cute in his Moses robe, satin sash, and kukui nut lei, I gotta go church for see him do his thing.

So all the kids walking down the middle aisle with their coffee filter kāhilis and my mother tell me, "Ho, look nice, yeah?" But get kinda plenty coffee filters falling out of the chicken wire. I tell my mother, "Ma, why you never just borrow the kāhilis from the church school? They get for May Day."

My mother's face kinda dropped and she neva say nothing.

I go, "You neva think of that?!"

That's why my mother had swear at me in church.

So from now on, no matter what I do, she cannot tell me nothing because I tell her, eh, at least I never use that kind language in the House of the Lord.

And you know what else? She no buy coffee filters no more. She shame. She use paper towel.

LISA KAMA

—

IN THE SNACK AISLE

YOU KNOW HOW HARD IT IS TO FIND PICKLED MANGO?
Get dried mango, li hing mango, sweet mango mui or whatevers, but I
talking green mango, vinegar juice, red food coloring, jar with little bit rust
on the metal lid.

I so ono for pickled mango.
I cannot tell you how ono I am for pickled mango.

I can eat one whole jar pickled mango all by myself. One time.
I can eat pickled mango until my lips are peeling and my tongue is numb
and the roof of my mouth has blisters.
I can eat pickled mango for breakfast and wash it down with a glass of milk.
I can eat pickled mango on bread for lunch.
I can eat pickled mango with rice for dinner.
I can get up in the middle of the night and eat pickled mango, brush my
teeth and go right back to sleep.
I can suck the vinegar juice right from that rusty metal lid.

I know I can, cuz I already did.
And I like more.

When my Mom was pregnant with me, she ate Samoan can tuna
breakfast, lunch, and dinner. She ate Samoan can tuna the way I eat pickled
mango. My aunty-them had to ship 'em in for her. But Samoan can tuna
easier to find than pickled mango.

With my sister, it was chocolate. Her husband had to hide all the candy in the house, but she would find it. He had to hide the car keys because she would sneak out in the middle of the night. He'd find her sleeping in the car at Safeway, all Hershey's wrappers by her feet and one big smile on her face.

I heard had pickled mango at one store Wahiawā. I made my husband drive me.
We get there, the place closed.
I tell him break the window.
He tell me this gotta stop.

So Longs is my last hope.
And if they no more on the shelves, I going just walk up and down the aisles and ask every clerk and every customer if they get green mangoes their house and if they tell yeah I going ask, where you live? We go!
I cannot tell you how ono I am for pickled mango.

DEREK Y.Y. PANG
–
PROFESSIONAL THUG

HERE YOU ARE.
I thought I would find you in the Tylenol aisle.
Oh, no, you not going check out yet.
We going have a little talk, first.

I can unnastan you no mo da money, but what I no can unnastan is how come you telling me you no mo da money.
Look at me.
Check my size, bra.
How's my girth?

You like dat word, eh? Girth.
That means wide.
They use that word when they talking about horses.
They use that word when they talk about me.
Girth.
I get girth.
I wide,
like one horse.

So das why I cannot unnastan why you, one small pitot, mejiro bird little guy stay looking at me wid all my girth and telling me you no mo da money.
You supposed to be begging.
You supposed to be crying.

You supposed to be telling me all kind lies, like you going get da money as soon as your braddah sell his car or as soon as the check clear da bank or as soon as your chick give you back da bracelet.

You supposed to be telling me stuff like, "No, Mr. Pang! I had the money, but then one guy more big den you came and took 'em!" That's what you supposed to be doing.

But for stand there, look me straight in da eye and tell me to my face you no mo' da money, I cannot believe.

I cannot think.

Neva happen to me in all my years in the collection industry.

You with all your nerve, me with all my girth.

UNCLE CHOOCHIE NAWAI

–

SHOP STEWARD

HELLO? HELLO? HELLO? FUCK IT. HELLO? WHO DIS? DIS
Choochie, who dis?

I stay Longs.

Longs.

LONGS!

Why, who dis? Who dis? Who? Dis you or I got wrong number?

Eh, Bobby, das you?

How come you get one drug dealer voice when you say hello?

What is "yo"?

Das not how you answer phone.

You sound like one drug dealer. I thought you was one drug dealer. Never
mind. Never mind I said.

DRUG DEALER!

Shit, you making me shame in Longs, Bobby. No make me shame in Longs.

Go ask Mommy what kind she like.

Go ask Mommy what kind she like.

What brand.

Go ask.

No, not color, it's what brand.

No, not what flavor. The thing no come in flavor. I no think the thing come
in flavor.

What brand. Find out the brand Bobby. Get like choke brands that kind and I no like get the wrong one, bumbye gotta come back. Find out the brand.

Da what?

What?

No more that kind.
No more.
I need the brand Bobby.
Shit, I coming shame already, Bobby.
People looking.
They looking.
I stay inside the wahine aisle at Longs yelling at my damn drug dealer kid on one small piece plastic dat play da Lone Ranger song when supposed to ring like one RING.
Help me out, Bobby, what's the brand?

What's the brand!

Go talk to your mother and find out what is the god damn brand so I can grab the thing, run to the car and dig the hell out of here before one of the guys from my working place see me.

FIND OUT THE FUCKING BRAND!!!

Okay, now ask her what size.

NADINE AND THE OLD MAN
WITH THE PĪKAKE

*E*VERY MORNING EIGHT O'CLOCK SHARP, HE COME IN WITH his plastic bag full with pīkake. If not in bloom, he bring gardenia, but then he apologize about the bugs. If no more flowers his house, he bring plumeria from the school, but then he look little bit shame. Like maybe not so good. He put the plumeria on toothpick and go right down the row and give to all the girls. That's his thing. He come to flirt with the girls. Pretty good for one old fut, I tell Sonya. She tell sad, yeah, since he lost the wife. Sometimes when no more flowers his yard or windy, he bring papaya. Anything just so he can go down the line and say hi to all us. Sometimes, when he get extra, he give the girls at Bank of Hawaii next door or he make us two, one to put in our hair, one to put by our registers.

Come to find out, get one at every Longs. Every store get their own old man who bring flowers from his yard. Sometimes they still get the wife, but she real quiet or she don't leave the house. Mostly, the wife is gone already and they just get their yard. And us.

Not like we get time to talk story. Maybe he get for come behind the counter to put the flower in our hair. Maybe he get one small half-hug. Hard, 'cause we so busy. And not like he ever buying anything. When Sonya working, she see him coming, she run fast in the back, get him one cup coffee. If get pastry in the break room, she give that, too. Ho, his face is like he hit the jackpot. I tell her ho, Sonya, you so nice. She tell me, stupid, he the one being nice. I just getting him some damn coffee and one stale doughnut.

CHERYL MOANA MARIE SAKATA
–
KAIMUKĪ

SO I'M SITTING ON THE BENCH AT ZIPPY'S WAITING FOR MY large chili cracka and thinking if I gotta stop Foodland still yet on the way home and what was on sale at Longs this week and then it hits me:

My whole life is Zippy's, Foodland, Longs.
Zippy's, Foodland, Longs.

Sometimes, the order change little bit.
If I buying stuff like ice cream or frozen chicken, I go Foodland last.
Or if I pick up the kids, then I do my shopping first and take them Zippy's after.
But other than those variations, that's it.

Longs, Zippy's, Foodland.
Foodland, Longs, Zippy's.
Zippy's, Foodland, Longs. Zippy's, Foodland, Longs.

And I tried to think when my life wasn't Zippy's, Foodland, Longs.
Before I had kids,
before I got married,
before I got married again.

Small kid time, same thing.
Instead of Zippy's, we went Diners and instead of Foodland my mada had Tamashiro's down the street.
But Longs was Longs.

I think there was like this short time in between high school and the first
baby when I actually went to a real restaurant.
Not like Sizzler or Wailana, but the kind with tablecloth.
I remember thinking that it took a really long time for the food to come,
but nobody else looked pissed off so I figured that's just how it is.
I guess so people who go to real restaurants have the time.
They don't have to run to Foodland and Longs after.

And as I'm sitting there, trying to think how many years of my life I've spent
sitting on a bench at Zippy's waiting for my damn chili cracka, it hits me
again, but this time, it's even worse.
This is my whole life.
This is the rest of my life.
Zippy's, Foodland, Longs.
Zippy's Foodland Longs.

When I'm an old, old lady and can hardly walk, going be the same thing:
Zippy's, Foodland, Longs,
Zippy's, Foodland, Longs.

Except, going be real early in the morning.

II.

BABES, WHY YOU ACKING LI'DAT FOR?

ROGELIO CABINGABANG
A.K.A. "DJ STANKMASTER"

*B*ABES, WHY YOU ACKING LI'DAT FOR? HA? WHY YOU ACKING li'dat?

You know I love you babes.

You my babes.

You my only babes, babes.

My odda babes befo', she no was my babes. Not like you my babes, babes.

Ho, babes, when I go sleep at night, I close my eyes and I only see you, babes.

When I dream, I dream of you, babes.

I wake up in the morning, I open my eyes, I only see you babes.

I see you and I wonder how you snuck out your house without your father catching you and giving you dirty lickens, but I see you, babes. I come all happy.

You know why? Cuz you my babes, 'as why.

You remember the time Sheldeen-dem called you one bitch and you got suspension six days fo' throwing her sister through the girls' bathroom window?

I had back you up, babes.

All the way.

The whole time you was home, I neva even talk to one nodda girl. Notting. Even when Mrs. Sakata made me partner with Tiana Muñoz for Social Studies class, I neva talk to her notting.

She not my babes 'as why.

You my babes.

She not my babes.
I mean she used to be my babes befo' time, but she not my babes no
more.
No ways.

Not even when you get suspension,
not even when you got arrested,
not even when you got charged attempted murder and had to go juvenile
detention two nights befo' they found out wasn't your fingerprints on the
cricket bat.
No ways.

Even if I had to go Tiana's house every night fo' make study partner fo'
Mrs. Sakata's class, you always is my one and only babes, babes.
And when Tiana WAS my babes, befo' time, she no was really my babes,
you know?
Not like how you my babes.
Ho babes,
you my babes.

Always and forever.

Babes.

CRAZY AUNTY COOKIE
—
USED TO BE MARRIED INTO THE FAMILY BUT STILL COMES TO PARTIES

YOU KNOW HOW YOU READ THE MAGAZINES AND THEY tell you how to tell about a man? Like "How Your Man Drinks Coffee Tells You What Kind of Partner He'll Be" or "What's in a Man's Car Reveals the Kind of Lover He Is."

What is that? I mean, how he act going tell you what kinda partner a man is, right? And if you like know what kinda lover he is, well, what can I say, you gotta sample before you buy, yeah?

But how he drink coffee, what he get in his car, the lines he get on his hand, the moles he get on his back, that don't tell you nothing. That's not how.

I tell you, but. The one thing you gotta look is how one man rips tape. You laughing now, yeah, but I promise, how he handle one roll pack-and-seal is very revealing.

Not like I made research study or anything, but I did work Island Movers couple-tree years, and I got to know some of the boyz real good. Real good.

Like Jerry, he was the wild one. How you call, impulsive. He would rip the masking tape with his teeth. SSSSHHHHAAAA! Exciting, you know. But after a while, not so good.

Some guys, they use the two-handed twist method. Too much work, that kind, and plenny times, they leave that long tape tail, you know the jagged one keeps going around and around and around the roll. Hard to get rid of that kind. No good. Sometimes gotta start up one whole new roll. Humbug.

Then get the guys use knife for cut the tape. Or more worse, scissors. What's up with that? They no like touch? No like get their hands sticky? I don't think so.

Sometimes, you see the guys use two-hand twist, teeth, knife, scissors, everything but they still get the tape all twist-up, stuck to their hands, tangle up everything. No waste your time, sistah. No waste your time.

What you like look for is one man can tear off the tape one stroke with just his thumbnail. Fffftt! Clean. No rough edges. Smooth. That's the one. That's the winner. Just put the sticky part on the box, pull down, and fft, one hand. Maybe he use the odda hand for stick 'em on good. Whoo, boy. That's the one. That's the one.

KAIPO BALMORES

—

NEWLY SINGLE

SO ME AND MY GIRLFRIEND, WE WAS WALKING AROUND Longs and she was laughing up cuz I was making like I in the Society of Seven, like maybe I numba eight, the second team . . . cuz you know they get about twenty-one guys on the bench and they just switch around like football.

So she was cracking up and just so happens we was coming around by the light bulb/extension cord aisle and I seen this girl and I couldn't help it and before I could even think my mouth just went "Ho!"

And wasn't just the kind "Ho" kind "Ho." Was the kind "HO!" kind "Ho." And the girl heard me go "HO!" and she had turn around. And she was pissed. And my girlfriend, she heard me go "HO!" except she thought was the kind "Ho" kind "Ho," so she stop laughing right there and could tell she was pissed, too.

So there I am in the towel rack and plunger aisle of Kaimukī Longs and I get one piss off one in front of me and one piss off one behind. And I thinking, "Ho!"

I just like Jackie Chan over the shelf into the Kleenex and toilet paper aisle already.

So while I trying fo' figure out if I could clear the Igloo coolers on the top shelf, my girlfriend takes the shopping cart and heads straight to the check-out counter. And I kinda tripping out because we didn't even get the paper towels and hashi on sale yet and going check out already, pushing the cart with the buss-up wheel,

Kaduk-kaduk-kaduk.

I walk by her, she go more fast.

Kaduk-kaduk-kaduk.

So I tell her, "What?" and she go, "Notting," and I go, "Not notting, what?" And she told me, "I heard you go HO," and I tell her, "I neva go HO," and she's like, "I heard you go HO," and I told her, "Yeah, I went HO but I neva go HO." And she go, "Same difference."

Kaduk-kaduk-kaduk.

So I stay thinking, wow, should I just give it all up and explain or is that going get me in more trouble. So I decide just fo' go for it. I tell her, "I went HO not like she pretty. I went HO cuz that girl, she get one really big ass."

My girlfriend's eyes got all big. I figure I had to swim fast or I was going eat it. I told her, "Beyonce big. Bootylicious big. Like one Sir Mix-A-Lot video big." And my girlfriend's eyes got all small and she tell me, "You told me that about me. You said that's the kind you like."

And the thing came out of my mouth before I could even think: "Yeah, but her ass even way more big than yours."

Just so happens, Beyonce was standing right there in the next check-out line and she had hear. I could see her gunning with her buss-up shopping cart:

Tang-tang-tang.

So I hang around the hair dye/razor blades aisle for twenty minutes, trying fo' decide if safe, listening if the shopping cart leaving the store:

Kaduk kaduk kaduk.

Tang-tang-tang.

When I finally walk out to the parking lot, I see my car, windows smash, tires flat, doors dented. So the cop ask me if I get one description of the suspect. I tell 'em, yeah, she piss off and she get one big ass.

LEONARD KAUI

—

DONNA'S OLDER BROTHER

DONNA USED TO BE PRETTY BEFORE. EVEN NOW, SOMETIMES when you look at her when she not thinking, you can still kinda tell little bit. But then juss like one thought fly through her mind like one mosquito in the night and she go back to looking juss how she always look.

She neva come that way when she got sick, you know. She was like that before.

She got sick because she came that way. She look at herself in the mirror and that made her sick. Sound like I joking but I not. That's how your brain work sometimes. You make yourself for real sick because you make yourself sick. You understand?

I tried to tell Donna that, but her, cannot tell her nothing.

She smart girl, her, but not smart for figure out some stuff. Not about her own self. She smart for understand math and numbers but something go wrong inside her life and she only think think think and she neva come out with the answer.

We used to tell her that some things, cannot understand. They just happen. Nobody know why. But she no like hear that. She don't believe in that. So her brain think on top of itself and that's how come she came like that and that's how come she look like that and that's how come she came sick.

So when you talk to her, don't mention nothing, 'kay? Nothing she can worry about. Nothing she gotta think think think.

LINDA HAMAMOTO

—

BANK WORKER

NO LOOK AT ME LIKE I CRAZY CUZ I KNOW YOU DO IT TOO.

You lonely.

You start thinking about
. . . stuff.

You start getting those
. . . feelings.

Some of my friends, they go bar or club or 24-Hour Fitness.

Me, I go McKinley Car Wash.

You mean to tell me you never did take notice the way those guys rub the cars?
Whack the mats?
Use the hose?
Come on.
I know I not the only one.

My car not even dirty and I go there on my lunch break.

The big braddah with the jail house tattoos and the buss teeth come up to me and ask me what I want.

I tell 'em, Junior, I like you fill 'em up.
I like you fill 'em up and then I like you wash 'em
and yeah I like the wax.
Give me the wax, Junior.
I like dat wax.

Sometimes, I tell the guy that I think so I spilled my cigarette ashes under
the seat so that he gotta go with the vacuum hose way way underneath
and then I stand right in the back of him and,
on a good day,
I get, like,
four inches of ono.

See, those guys, they look bad. I like that.
They look bad, but they get job.
I like that even more.

KELCIE CAMARA
—
CLERK ON BREAK

*I*LOOKING AT HIM AND I CANNOT BELIEVE WHAT HAD JUST
come out of his mouth
but I trying not for look like I cannot believe
but hard
because I cannot believe.

And he just looking at me,
waiting for me say something,
looking like I going say something,

but I cannot say nothing.
I cannot think.
I trying for be cool
but I cannot believe.

And me,
the whole time before that time I was all talking, talking, acting, acting like
been there, done that.
But what he had ask me,
I never been there and I would never even think to do that.
Who would do that?
I don't know nobody.
Except maybe that chick Wanette down in receiving.
She look like she would.

She look like she did.

And here him, looking at me,
looking looking. Waiting waiting.
And I stay trying, trying, holding, holding,
no like crack,
no like him know that I never did in my whole life even hear of nothing like that
but gotta act cool like I did,
oh yeah, sure, me? All the time. Why? No big deal. That's how.
But ai-ya
I no can believe.

And my mind is all white,

like when you go to the bathroom in the middle of the night and you turn
on the light.
AAAAH!
How the hell? I cannot even picture.
I really and truly
no can believe.

So finally, he tell me,
"You like or what?"
and me,

I cannot believe what had come out of my mouth.

I wen tell him,
"Yeah."

I no can believe.

DELORES KINORES

—

ONLY BUYS COFFEE ON SALE

HAVING SEXUAL RELATIONS WITH TOO MANY MEN WILL GIVE you cancer and wrinkles.

Having sexual relations when you are too young, like younger than twenty-five, will give you cancer.

Having sexual relations when you are not married will give you diseases and itches worse than cancer.
And it will give you cancer.

The tricky thing is, though, if you don't ever have sexual relations or not enough, you will get cancer that way, too.

But not the wrinkles.

My friend Sophie—three times married and boyfriends always on the side.
She died of cancer last June.
Face like a pickled plum.

My friend Julie,
married at sixteen,
grandmother at thirty because, you know, her daughter ended up just like her.
She was dead by forty-two.
Cancer.

My friend Junko,
she had cancer, too,
but it was the stroke that killed her.
Never married, never fooled around.
Died with the face of an angel. Not a single line.
But she still died.

Me, I'm looking younger ever since Vincent passed away.
Doctor says I'm in excellent health. Passed all my tests.
Vincent was the one caught the cancer.

But men, they get 'em different way.
It's what they breathe in their lungs,
like where they work or if they smoke,
and it's what they eat if it's bad food.

Men get their cancer from up side.
Doesn't matter too much what they do down there.

ANNA SIMAO
–
JOHNNY'S EX

I DON'T KNOW HOW MANY TIMES I'VE SAID I SHOULD HAVE known. But I should have known.

I should have known from the very first time I met him, he had this smell, like he wiped himself with a bath towel that no one washed for a couple months. He had that stink towel smell. Somewhere in my mind, I thought, poor thing. He needs a woman to wash his towels for him. Here's someone I can take care of.

When we met, he told me he was a pro surfer and when I said no kidding, my cousin is a pro surfer too. Maybe you folks know each other. Oh, all of a sudden he USED to be a pro surfer but then he had an accident so he doesn't surf so much any more. At least not pro.

And then he tells me that he's a businessman. So I go what kind of business? And he says he owns his own business. And I go what kind? And he says, well, he has several. Auto parts, construction, carpentry, welding. So I thought, wow, talented. Stupid yeah? And I felt so sorry when he told me one of his employees stole money from him and a lot of his equipment and now the jobs are backed up and his companies are in debt so I just had to help him make rent on the office, just one month, okay, two months, just to help, you know. Because I'm that way. I figure if they ask and if I can help, then I try to do the right thing. But that's how they trick you. They get you to think you're doing the right thing.

He tells me because the business is in trouble and because he really wants to pay me back, he has to work nights. All night. He says he's willing to make that sacrifice. And I say, that's okay. Just come over when you're done.

And I give him a key.

And pretty soon, he's sleeping at my house all day while I go to work, gone by the time I come home. And I never see him. But I can smell him on my sheets. I could smell him on my towels.

I should have known.

I should have known, but after everything that happened, I know better. It wasn't the towel that was making him stink. It was him stinking up the towel.

JAMES KIMO HOOPAI
—
THE BEST JAWAIIAN SONG EVER WRITTEN

I SAT IN MY TRUCK
And I wrote you dis song
Fo tell you I love you
And fo say I wuz wrong

I sorry I hurt you
I sorry I had lie
When I saw you hurtin'
Ho, I just had like die

I no could go surfing
I no could go eat
I no could go sleep
Ho, I just felt like shet

When I close my eyes
I can just see your face
All mad with my ass
And flying my stuff every place

If you come back to me
I not going do 'em again
So please listen to me
And no listen your friend

I going treat you real good

Like how I would say
Only this time, you watch
You not going find Raynette Dutro's panties in my glove compartment

So if you like my song
Please come back to me
I still waiting in my truck
Because you took da key

ENOLA VARGAS
—
TRYING TO HIT HER FIVE YEARS WITH THE COMPANY

*F*RIDAY NIGHT, WE GO GIRLS' NIGHT OUT. TALK, DRINK, LAUGH up like we best friends. Monday morning, I walk in the break room. Boop! Everybody get quiet.

Okay then. Fine. That's how you want to play it, well alright. I go back to my desk. I try to focus on my work but I'm thinking, what? Like I was the one dancing on the table showing panty to the waiter. Like I was the one riding the parking meter like a bucking bronco going "Naughty horsey! Naughty horsey!" Like I was the one so drunk I was barfing in my handbag.

Yeah, Denise. Yeah, Wanda. Yeah, Cookie. Go ahead and act because I remember everything.

Around 10:30 I like get coffee but they're still inside the break room so I go inside my purse to grab some quarters from the bottom for the soda machine and, whoa. What is that?

Oh man. Oh man. No tell me that was ME.

Shet. Was.

Wanda the one bought all those damn bloody Jell-O shots, lying, like, "It's not alcohol. It's only Jell-O! And sugar free!"

So I got a little wild. Not like I was the only one being happy while they were all in church.

I tell Wanda, so what? She says, "You kind of had a lot to drink." I go, so I got a little loose. So what? She goes, "You peed in a shot glass." Couldn't have been THAT drunk if I can aim in a shot glass, right. She goes, "You missed."

Now I gotta buy new shoes.

This goes on for a week. Whisper whisper in the break room. I walk in—silence.

One whole week.

I went through all my coffee withdrawals because I couldn't get near the damn coffee pot.

The next week Monday comes, I make sure I go work early. Early, early, so I'm the first one there. I go inside the break room and I made a big pot of coffee. I even bought expensive coffee for them, the one comes in a bag, not a can. Ten cups. Measure it all out so it's just right. Then I fill the water, not from the break room sink, not from the bathroom sink, from the toilet water. And I not talking the water from the tank. I'm talking bowl. But I shishi little bit inside first. Just a little. Just a pshht! Like when you nervous. And I fill the water and set that baby to go.

When they come in, they tell me, Enola, you made the coffee? It's delicious! I tell them thank you. Aren't you having any?

I tell them no, I watching what I drink.

JUNIOR

—

FROM McKINLEY CAR WASH

*E*H! DEA HER! DAS DA ONE!
Look look look look look.
Oh wait, no look. No let her catch you looking, but look when she not looking.

No let her get in my line.
Ah, she in your line!
I sorry braddah.

I feel sorry for you.

Okay, just no make eye contact and when you go for vacuum the car, tell her she gotta get out first. Say it's regalations. Or else she just going sit there in the passenger seat, make you stick the hose in between her legs and I sorry, but she nasty. And she not wearing nothing underneath that skirt so if you make accident, you going get fired so just focus on the floor.

When you get to the back seat, keep one hand on the vacuum hose and one hand on the back of your pants. Or else she going look your crack and I sorry, but that's nasty. I no like no somebody's mother looking at me like that. That's not right.

When you wash the windows, no look inside because that's when she going try flash you. So no look and if you accidentally look, no make big eye otherwise she just going do 'em more.

Sick yeah? Why she don't go bar or something? Why she don't go gym. She get bucks. Look how nice her car. Sometimes she come three times in one week. Her car not even dirty and she come.

She old like my mother already. In fact, I think so she get kids because one time I found a Happy Meal box underneath the seat. Sick eh? She come here catch her jollies off all us. And you know her, she no even leave tip. That's the worse. She get bucks. Look her car. And you should see her house.

Eh, just watch out that lady.
Never mind already.
I do 'em.

RANDY KAMA

—

LOYAL FRIEND

NO NO NO NO. HON, I NOT GOING VEGAS JUST ME AND Chala. Noreen going to.

What? No get mad at me.

Chala taking Noreen. What?! They getting married. She neva tell you? They is. They are. Them two. And me. I mean, not me. I married to you. At least for now I am.

Just listen to me already.

No, cuz Chala like take Noreen up Vegas when they get married. They getting married here, but. Not up there. Noreen like get married in front the judge so she can save money for the reception. She neva say nothing to you? Because I think so she was going ask you help with the party favors.

What?! No get mad at me about that one.

Noreen YOUR friend. I neva tell her tell you for help make party favors. I don't know. She neva say nothing to you yet so maybe she not going ask you. She asked all Wanda-them from work, but.

What?! No get mad at me for that. That's Noreen asking Wanda-them. Not me.

Wait, you like Noreen ask you make party favors or you no like Noreen ask you make party favors?

No tell me, tell her. You wahines work 'em out.

OK, so about Vegas, we going. Them two and me. They going for they honeymoon. Chala like me go for show him da ropes.

Not that kind ropes, damn it. Not that kind ropes. Eh, no laugh. I know that kind ropes and I could show 'em if I like. But I no like. That's my own damn ropes and you better stop laughing.

Chala like me show them around Vegas. They never did go Mainland. Not even high school band time because Chala was academic suspension that time and he no could go with all us.

Chala like me show them how because he no like get lost. They get hard time understand how Mainland people talk. I told him, Mainland is hard because they no mo mauka. They no more 'Ewa. You know what I'm saying?

And they scared the hotel. They no believe get new towels every day and don't gotta fix the bed. They like bring hot plate to cook in the room. I told them no be so country jack. The water from the bathroom come hot enough to make Cup Noodles.

So going be them two on their honeymoon and me. You understand, right? They going to have fun. I going to help them. I figure you no like go because you get the kids. I would ask you if you like go but I know you still mad cuz we never made our honeymoon yet and I keep saying we going. And we going. We going. But this trip is Noreen and Chala-dem's honeymoon. I just going for help out.

BERNETTA DE COITO
—
STILL WEARS STIRRUP PANTS

WHEN I FIRST MET HIM, I THOUGHT HE WAS SO ROMANTIC. I was working that time at the club and he used to come in, talk story with me.

At first was just hi, how are you, how you doing, but then he started putting on his moves.

One time he brought me one red rose with one long ribbon. I thought he was so cool. A single red rose. Back then, I was too dumb to figure out, yeah, a single red rose because he was too cheap to buy the other eleven.

He never did tell me that he love me. He would always say it like, "Babes, I would give my left nut if I could hold your hand." Or "Babes, I would give my left nut for one kiss from your lips." When me and him got married, was, "Babes, I would give my left nut if you would be my wife."

Me, I was all in heaven with this guy. I mean, one guy telling you he would give one nut for you, you must be special. More special than one nut.

I don't know if left side better or worse or same, but one nut is one nut, and he was saying he would give 'em for me.

I felt bad I neva have nuts for give to him.

But after a while, I started for notice. I started for notice all the little things that you no really let yourself notice in the beginning part when they bringing you roses and giving out nuts.

I took notice how every morning, first thing, he scratch his ʻōkole then he rub his nose. I took notice always get about twenty dollars missing from my tip money. I took notice he jump for grab his pager when the thing go off, and then fast he gotta leave the house for go buy cigarettes, no come home until three-four o'clock in the morning.

And I took notice he was giving out his nuts left and right.

Left and right.

"I would give my left nut for dat Mercedes."

"I would give my left nut the Packers make it to the play-offs."

"I would give my left nut for go Vegas."

"I would give my left nut for one more beer."

That last one, that's the one. I heard that, I had snap. I thought I was special. More special than one left nut. And here he was giving one left nut for another beer and he stay three steps away from the cooler and he know get planny more Bud inside.

You would, eh? You would, eh? You would? Give your left nut? For one beer?

Then hea. Hea. Hea you like your Bud, take 'em!

Take your beer! You like 'em, take 'em! Take em! Take em! TAKE 'EM!!!

. . . NOW PAY!

III.

BACK TO SCHOOL

MARCUS S. MORIKAWA
–
PRINCIPAL

*Y*ES, WE ARE FULLY AWARE OF THE CONTRIBUTIONS YOU AND your husband have made to the annual fund-raiser. We couldn't have made the beef stew without your pigs. But the thing is your son's behavior has become, well, something of a problem.

Take for example the run-in he had with Ms. Kimata. Now, we understand your son is excitable, but it took a team of surgeons five hours to remove the pencil. Ms. Kimata hasn't been able to return to the classroom yet. She'll be in rehab for many months.

Then there was the occurrence on the school bus. Yes, we realize there is often rowdy behavior at this age, but the police have had that bus impounded for three months now gathering evidence and there's a lot of students who are having to walk a long way to get to school.

Last week, it was the incident with Mrs. Ishikawa, and while we know she is one of our, shall we say, less affectionate janitors, she did not deserve what your son did to her with the mop. And the thing with the Mr. Clean, well, we think you'd have to agree, that was over the top.

And today. We waited until the last possible moment to call you in. Believe me, we tried everything we could think of, but he's had those third graders locked in the cafeteria for five hours now and their parents are getting a little bit worried. We thought maybe you could try to talk to him. Let him know everything's okay. And tell him don't worry about the fire. We needed a new library anyway.

Thanks. Thank you. Very much. So sorry to have to call you in like this. We know it's a real hassle for you. It's just that your son is a . . . very spirited child, and quite strong for a first grader.

RENNY RENALDO

—

FORMER ATHLETE AND MOTIVATIONAL SPEAKER

*E*VERYBODY FEELING ALL RIGHT RIGHT NOW? ALL RIGHT!

First of all, I want to thank the students and teachers of this school for inviting me to speak here to the students and teachers of this school.
All right? Say all right!
All right.
It's always a big honor for me to talk to the youths of today, because like I always say, you are our future and we won't have any tomorrow without your today.
All right?
All right.

I spend a lot of time talking to kids just like you, kids who are troubled, kids who have trouble, kids who are in trouble, and sometimes, I meet some really troubled kids, and that troubles me, but this is my way of giving back and in that way, it's no trouble at all.

Whenever I come to a school like this, I talk to the students and try to give them hope by talking to them, giving them hope, telling them about the power of their dreams, and let me tell you, it's a beautiful thing when you see a young person hoping and dreaming. Put your hands together for that.
All right.

I know you folks might have problems. We all have problems. I myself have had problems in my life. Some people have a hard time believing that, but it's true. But when you have a problem or problems, because sometimes problems come all at once and that's a real problem—you have to remember, problems are never as big as the dreams you have inside, so you always have to have a dream, no matter how small. As long as you believe and have hope, you will have a dream. It took me a long time to learn that, but I wanted to share that with you now. All right.

It was always my dream to tour the State of Hawai'i speaking in high school auditoriums and sharing my message of hope with students like yourself, so I'd like to thank you for making that dream come true for me. All right. I'd also like to thank my sponsors, Seki Electronics, Tamura's Body and Fender, and the State Department of Business, Economic Development, and Tourism for their generous support of my volunteer work. All right for that!

I leave you now with my motto. It's what I tell all my kids, because I don't have kids of my own so I think of all of you as my hundreds of adopted children, I tell them remember the three important things in life, the three things that will always get you ahead. Say it with me, now: Reading is good, drugs is bad, use a condom. Again, reading is good, drugs is bad, use a condom.

All right!

KALANI DOMINGO

–

RULES

*T*HESE ARE THE THINGS YOU CANNOT DO:

—Cut your fingernails at night.
—Whistle at night.
—Sing Christmas songs when it's not Christmas.
—Run with scissors, but that's different because it's not a bad luck thing, except if you got stabbed because you were running with scissors or if you stabbed somebody, which would be bad luck, sorta.
—Break a mirror or you get seven years bad luck plus you get three years of bad luck just by running and playing by a big mirror or throwing the ball anywhere near.
—Bring bananas to the beach.
—Tell somebody you're going fishing. Not because you're going to die but because the fish will hear and they'll go someplace else.
—Stick a scissors behind the door (I don't know about this one but that's what my mom said although I don't know why you would stick a scissors behind a door unless you were hiding it fast because you almost got caught running).
—Point in a graveyard and if you do, you have to bite your finger.
—Sweep at night, which my sister extends to late afternoon so she doesn't have to do her chores.
—Sweep the dirt out the door because you'll sweep out all your money.
—Write your name along with a girl's name and put "4-ever" because "4-ever" breaks you up. Unless that's what you want.
—Eat and then swim too soon, but that's not a bad luck thing either. That's a you-might-get-a-cramp-and-drown thing.

—Turn your back to the ocean because it's disrespectful. And a wave could knock you down.

—Eat the tip of a piece of pie, but that's not a bad luck thing, too. That's a good luck thing if you leave that part until last and then make a wish.

—Laugh at somebody when something bad happens to them because then that something bad will happen to you.

That's most of the things you have to do and not do. There are more but I can't remember. But if you do and don't do those things, you should be okay.

JOHN TAFUA

—

MOVED BACK FROM MAINLAND

WHEN HE FIRST CAME TO THE HOUSE, I THOUGHT HE WAS a monster. It wasn't just how he looked. It was in everything he did. He drank milk from the milk carton even when my mother was watching. He used dirty words even when he wasn't mad. He took things. Hid things. Broke things.

My mother told me I had to be kind to him because he didn't grow up in a house like ours. He wasn't used to the way we lived. I wasn't used to the way he lived. To be honest, he scared me; and if I was in any way kind, it was only out of fear.

I couldn't even look at him for the longest time. He was covered with bumps. Totally misshapen. It was like he was warped and bubbling with anger. I stole glances when he watched TV.

At night I could hear him making noises. I stuck my fingers in my ears so that I couldn't hear to find out if he was crying. I mean, I knew he was, but I just couldn't think about it because that was worse than him being so mean.

As time passed, things changed. He got better. I got worse. He got nicer. I got mad. The better he got, the more I hated him. He took everything that used to be mine, including my golden reputation.

I became the monster.

I was the monster who could hear someone cry and keep perfectly still. I was the monster who couldn't be happy for someone's newfound happiness.

His bumps went down. I thought he had a disease. They were bee stings. They got infected. My mother said he came from a rough home.

His bumps went down and he stopped drinking from the milk carton and he made my father laugh at dinner and one day he was gone. Just gone. I think of him every time I have to fill out the "next of kin" line on a medical form. I wonder what he puts on that line. Not my name. But when I think who I have left, he's always the first that comes to mind.

MIKILEI BASA

—

WHAT IS CLASS

*T*HIS IS HOW I WANT TO MAKE MY WEDDING:
First, all the guys come in with horses.
No, first, going have my cousin Sheldyn blow the conch shell.
Then, going have the horses, all with leis and satin blankets.
And going be nice horses.
All white.
Not the mud puddle cow shit bird shit all kind shit in their tails horses that
my uncle Tommy get.
White horses.
Princess horses.
But only the guys going ride horse because Lachelle my best friend maid-
of-honor got bucked off her ass that one time and now she scared. So my
side of the court gotta walk.

After the conch shell and the horses, going get the kāhili bearers. My family
got aliʻi blood, that's why. I not too sure which line but I know that we are
royal because that's what my grandmother said.

After the kāhili bearers, going get my nephew's ʻukulele band. He good,
you know. They took first place in the whole school last year.

Then comes the groom. If it's Kaipo, he don't ride horse but if I end up
marrying Clayton, he do. Clayton ride horse good.

Okay, then get all my maid-of-honor and my bridesmaids and my attendants and all my nieces will be flower girls so I hope my sister Jody don't pop out more daughters because I only like five or six flower girls.

And all my whole court going be wearing black—not the kind spooky funeral kind black but elegant black. Fancy black. Look nice that's why and not too much girls make their bridesmaids dresses black. Look nice but. And then the girls can use 'em when they go out and they not going bitch about "spend money, only wear the thing once." Plus, I get one cousin wear size zero, one other cousin in the how many X's size and one nodda cousin one side no more leg. What else color I going put them in but black?

And my dress going be all with satin top to bottom with rhinestones and lace and pearls. I drew one picture of how I like 'em inside my sophomore year math book but then I had to turn 'em in. So nice look. The back part is open so can see my butterfly tattoo and get little pants underneath in case I marry Clayton, then I can get on his horse after the vow part and me and him can ride away and cannot see my panty.

The best part is when they letta go the pigeons and they all fly over the monkeypod tree in the pasture.
So elegant, you know.
That is class.

RHONDALEI ALVARADO

–

TEEN BRUISER

*I*GOING CATCH THAT CHICK BY THE BATHROOM LUNCH recess time. You watch. She going get it. You no just walk around like how she walk around. You seen how she walk around? She lucky going be from me and not from Jenai Kaupe. That chick give some serious buss-ass, hair-on-the-ground, no-mo-teeth lickens. Me, when I pau, they still can walk. Not too good, but they can walk.

First time, Jenai Kaupe wen catch me by the bathrooms. I was walking around all tantaran just like that girl, and you no can walk around like that, but I neva know. Jenai had catch me by the bathrooms, but wasn't recess time when had people fo pull her off me or anything. Was first period, when had only me and her in the bathroom.

I was black and blue fo one whole month, you can believe?
I had to go hospital.
I had internal bleedings.
I lost couple teeth.
They wanted me to make police report but I neva tell nothing. Jenai thought was because I was scared fo give her name. She thought I neva like her catch me again. But me, I wasn't scared of her. I wanted her fo catch me in the bathrooms again.
That's how you learn.
That's how you come strong.

Jenai Kaupe took me out three times more. Took me that long fo learn. You see this scar over here and over here and this over here? That's all

70

from her. But that's how. The last time, I ripped her earring right off her ear, right through the puka. I had 'em in my hand, one gold hoop with one small piece ear on top. She just had look at me and that's how I knew was pau already.

That chick, walking around all da kine, she going learn today. Maybe take three, four, five times with her, but she going learn from me.
That kind, they gotta know how you supposed to walk around.

TRAYSEN SHIN

–

VARSITY

MY SCHOOL HAS THIS CARNIVAL, RIGHT? NOT A BIG ONE, but they do it every year for like a fund-raiser to buy, I don't know, stuff. And they make us go down and show face because we're on the team and first string and all that. Whatever. So stupid.

I get there and I'm expecting it to be lame, and then I see they have this dunking booth in the corner by the science building and who should be sitting up there on the plank but Mrs. Rodrigues, that fat cow who almost kept me off the team last year because she said I copied Jacob's test. Lucky I got more wrongs than him, or else the principal would have probably believed her and I would have spent my whole junior year riding the pine. That would have been it for my career. Mrs. Rodrigues hated me from the very start of school and after that happened, it was totally like hell in her class the whole rest of the year. I kept my mouth shut because I wanted to play, but I swore that I would get her back someday for being such a damn bitch to me when I didn't even do nothing.

I was thinking I was going to key her car or flat her tires, but this was even better. This was public. The whole school watching. Wanna go swimming Mrs. Rodrigues? Let me show you why I'm the captain of the team.

I had to borrow ten bucks from Alicia Silva, who will give me a rash of shit for the rest of my life but it will be so worth it. I paid my money and stood in line. A lot of guys wanted to dunk old Mrs. Rodrigues.

I did my warm-ups. Alicia watched and giggled with her friends. Crap, now she thinks there's something between us.

My friend Kainoa was the next in line. He's almost a better athlete than me but I have the speed, he has the strength. I didn't know he had trouble in Mrs. Rodrigues class but come to think of it, he was two hairs away from academic probation last year, too. I remember seeing him in study hall.

This is going to be great. Kainoa's rich, so he can buy lots of chances to dunk the old bitch. And he's got an arm on him.

The first ball flew out of Kainoa's hand and hit the tarp behind the target with a solid "whup!" Mrs. Rodrigues flinched, like maybe she was about to get beaned or shot and not just dunked in some water that had some leaves floating in it because of the wind.

I don't know why that bothered me but it did. That fat cow was sitting up there in shorts and a T-shirt over what must be the biggest old lady bathing suit Sears ever sold. Mrs. Rodrigues never wears shorts, not even to Athletic Day. Not even the long old lady shorts. Her legs were puffy and white with purple veins around her ankles. My grandma had that. It was gross and sick and nasty.

I told myself to remember her yelling at me in front of the whole class, like I was so dumb I had to copy off a dumb guy. She insulted me and threatened me. I got myself mad again.

The next ball Kainoa threw hit the target square, but Mrs. Rodrigues didn't go down. She flinched and her fat wiggly arms went up in the air in a panic, but she didn't fall. The lever on the booth must have gotten stuck.

Kainoa got mad, but he had a big smile on his face. "Not fair! Juice! Juice!" he yelled. He threw four more balls at the target really fast. Whap! Whap! Whap! Whap! They all hit but Mrs. Rodrigues didn't go down. "Too fat! The thing stuck!" Kainoa yelled.

He dropped the rest of the baseballs he was holding and charged the target. "No, no, no!" Mrs. Rodrigues said. Her voice made my stomach weird. She didn't sound like that when she was giving me hell.

Kainoa hit the target full-on with the weight of his body. The plank Mrs. Rodrigues was perched on dropped underneath her. There was this sick moment when she almost levitated above the water with nothing holding her up underneath her ass. Her hands were grabbing at nothing and her mouth was opening and closing like she was trying to give orders. And then, the biggest splash you ever saw. I heard her knees hit the bottom of the tank. Everyone cheered.

I gave Alicia back her stupid ten dollars and told her I'd drive her home from school one day. That made her way too happy.

JANESSA PERALTA
—
CORINNA'S FRIEND, SOMETIMES

DEAR JESUS PLEASE HELP ME NOT EAT SO GODDAMN MUCH because I can hardly fit in any of my new pants.

And Jesus please help me lose weight so that I don't look like such a goddamn cow in the prom pictures.

Jesus, please help me not fall asleep in math class because I'm flunking bad and if I have to go summer school I will be so shame.

Jesus, please make my mom come home late so she don't catch me with my face in a big bucket of chicken and call me a fat-a-boola and make me shame.

Please let her come home late and tired so that she doesn't even look in the fridge and doesn't even check in the garbage.

Please let me be pretty and slim and beautiful and never hungry or tired.

Please kick my ass so I exercise and not sit on the couch when I come home.

Jesus, please help me get through the day without thinking about lumpia or won ton or anything fried.

Please just let me think about other things.

Just fix my mind from thinking about what to eat.

Please help me lose weight even if I do eat.

Please bless my grandmother and make her stop fighting with my mother.

Please bless my brothers and my cousins.

Please bless my dad if he's still alive.

Bless that guy I hooked up with at the carnival the other night, Brayden or Branson or something.

Please bless my mom and make her tired so she doesn't notice anything.

And please bless me, Jesus. Please help me to not eat so goddamn much and to not swear because I'm sorry when I do.

Please.

Amen.

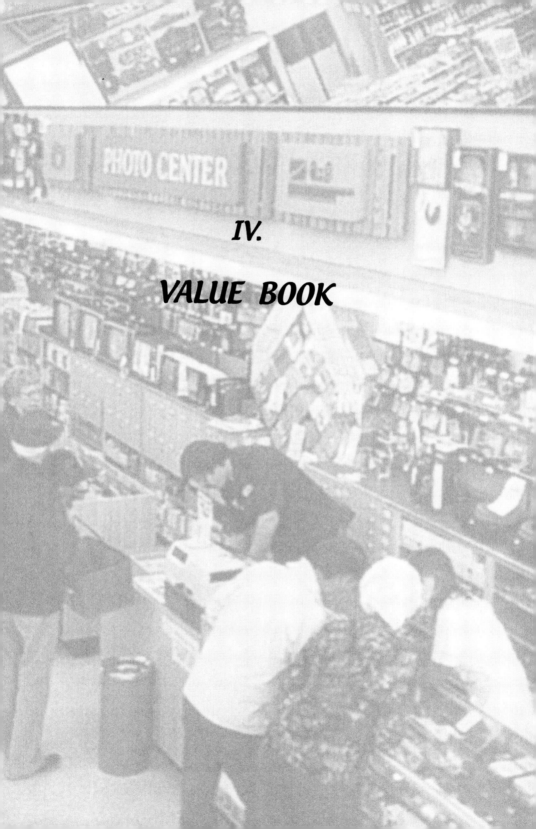

IV.

VALUE BOOK

NADINE TAM SING
—
NEVA GO BREAK YET

SO I GET FIFTEEN PEOPLE IN MY LINE AND I LOOKING around and Janet get maybe three and Sonya get maybe five so I trying to give the bag boy the eye like, eh, traffic management, but hard cuz none of us had our break yet so we all kinda tunnel vision and I get the guy.

Get one every shift.

This one, he like know what time the Wednesday sale items go on sale at the 24-hour Longs, of which this is not.

So I tell him, well, over here, our Wednesday sale items go on sale Wednesday, and I say 'em nice so I hoping that going be that.

But no.

Oh no.

He like me call the 24-hour Longs for find out for him.

I don't know what he like buy, but whatever he like get, it's so damn important to him he going plan his whole Tuesday night. Like if the answer is one minute after midnight, braddah going be there 11:30 pm just fo get ready.

So I call.

I get one friend work Pali so I call her over there, but I had forget her working schedule so I had to talk to the manager and take little while cuz they busy over there and I look my line and ho, maybe up to twenty people now and they all giving me the tapping the foot, crossing their arms, looking the watch.

So I finally get the answer for what time the Wednesday sale start at the 24-hour Longs and you know what the answer?

Five AM.

Shet.

PUKA-HEAD PACHECO

—

CONSPIRACY THEORIST

*S*HHHH. THEY WATCHING.

They always watching.

Look.

The cameras.

Over there.
Over there.
Over there, too.

They hide small little spy stuffs in the can green beans, braddah.

You take 'em home, they watch whatever you doing in your house.

They hide 'em in the can green beans 'cause they think that's the last place you would look.

But I wen look.
And I seen.
I seen them.
They seen me seen them.
They know I know.
That's why I no buy the green beans no more.

I had switch to canned asparagus.
No more taste and kinda tough, but at least no more the spy camera.
Plus, go on sale more often than the can green beans.

Oh, you no believe?
You think I mento?
Head case?
Paranoia da destroya?
Yeah, check this out.
I show you how they try jam up your brain.

Look the express check-out lane.

Go look.

Go look right now.

Look the sign.

Says "Nine Items or Less" right? Nine items or less.

Now look the jar candy.

The jar, the big plastic jar right there on the nine items or less check-out
counter.

Look the jar!

Look the sign on top.

What does the sign say?

Ten for dollar.

Now who crazy? Tell me that.

BOOGA SMYTH
–
LIVES UNDER BLUE TARP

PEOPLE SAY TO ME, THEY GO BOOGA, THEY SAY, WHY AND how come you talk the way you talk?

And I, Booga, tell them Booga talks like this because Booga thinks like this.
Booga is the full-package.
Talking, sounding, thinking, believing.
It's the full Booga, man.
Feeling, knowing, sensing, believing.
That's Booga, I tell them.
That is Booga and Booga is me.

What I don't tell them is that the clip is from the military.
They guess that the crush of words is from my time in, when there was no one to talk to and nothing to say.
But the clip, they don't pick that up right the way.
Military.
Not me, but my father.
Lifer, he was.
All the way through. Military man.
And he said it with the hard 't.' MiliTary.
That's the clip, so your talk is shiny as your shoes.

There's a thing that happens when you're raised that way.
You get to know your differences.
I, Booga, I got to know all my differences, all right.
I got to know my up from my down,

my left from my right,
my good from my bad,
my pass from my do-not-pass.
Un-ac-ceptable.
That word got a hard 't' in it, too.

Booga in his heart is not about no hard 't.'
Booga found that out early.
Booga is smooth.
Booga's loose.
Booga is . . . flow.

I been everywhere and I seen all kinds of differences and I chose my flow.

My father did not appreciate flow.
No he did not.
He did not like Boogaloo Boy at all.
NoT aT T'all.

He said Booga, thaT is whaT you call yourself, like the shiT you blow ouT
your nose.
Formless.
Useless.
DisgusTing.

My father was a man of few words.
Few, but with that hard clip that would nick and graze and cut.
CuT.

I, Booga, am a man of many words.
Booga is all about words.
Booga is all about flow.
I am the flow pushing and rounding smoothing out that hard, hard clip.

EDDIE GARCIA
–
MOODY M.F.

YOU EVER WALK AROUND YOUR HOUSE ALL PISS OFF, GOING and going and you so piss off with everything you cannot remember what you piss off about?

I tell you dis, I can get piss off like one chick.

I had plenty female influence my house growing up.
My sisters,
cousins,
my sisters' friends,
my mada,
my gramada,
all my step-madas and step-gramadas,
my mahu cousin Raymond.
I think so all that chickness just had rub off. I don't know how come I had to get the piss-off-ness instead of the cooking or the cleaning or the way for dress nice. But I think so that is what had happen.

I go work, somebody park little bit over the line by the parking space, I go off. Ruin my whole day. I no care they not parking where I like park. I get all mad. I get mad and then I gotta go around to all my co-workers and tell them about it. One at a time.

Get one new guy hired onto the job, I size the bugga up. Ay, he younger. Ay, he in shape. Ay, he make the boss laugh. Right there, I hate his guts. I catch myself talking shit about him and I don't even know the guy. Tell me that's not chick-style?

The worse, but, is when I catch somebody looking at me in a way or saying something to me in a way like they take notice I put on weight . . . like I order a beer and they go, "Light?" Ho, I go off. Like, what you saying? You calling me fat? I know you didn't just call me fat because nobody with an ass like that get any room for talk.

No get me wrong. I don't talk story four hours on the phone. I no like go shopping. I don't watch no ice skating. I one man, okay? And it ain't anger management issues because not like I throwing punches. It's only words and stink eye and sometimes the one-eyebrow action.

Here's the thing:
This is me.
Eddie Garcia.
And I'm a bitch.

JACKSON "BUTCHIE" FUNABIKI
—
STONE MASON AND ULUA FISHERMAN

I NO SLEEP GOOD.
My brain don't stop, that's why.
Cannot turn 'em off.

I think about all kind stuff.

I think about the jelly inside one can ham.
You know how when you go for open the can, get the jelly inside?
What is that?
And is ham jelly an accident or on purpose or some kind freak of nature?
And is Spam jelly same thing as ham jelly, cuz you know the Spam cans get
that too.
I cannot handle that jelly.
Gross.
All jelly, dat.
Sick.
Me, I wash my ham,
I wash my Spam.
Gotta.

If you look good, vienna sausage get that kind too, but not that much.

Maybe has to do with the weather or how long you keep 'em on the shelf.
I going try keep one can ham couple-three years,
and then get one new one from the store,
open 'em up both same time

and make experiment.

This is what is in my head when I lying on my air mattress in my mother-
guys living room.
I moved back home when my girlfriend kicked me out.
She tell me we no communicate and then she tell me I talk too much.
I tell her make up your mind.
She tell me, she did.

I think so what I looking for is peace of mind.
But then, I not sure what that means.
Do they mean peace of mind like you brains is all peaceful?
Or does it mean piece of mind like one small part or one piece or
something,
like I going give you a piece of my mind.

The thing is, my mind all jelly right now.
Jelly on top of ham.
And I cannot tell if that's how supposed to be
or if it's one freak of nature.

HARLAN CAMPOS
—
ON SUPERVISED RELEASE

HE GET HEART, THAT BOY. YOU SAW WHEN HE WALKED OFF the field? Could hardly walk, you saw? Was so swollen, they had to cut the shoe off. That's how they won the game. Thirty-two yards on a broken ankle. That's him. He neva let them carry him off the field. He would crawl first. That's how he is. From small-boy time. He no give up.

Before time, he used to do anything to come strong. He was lifting weights from fifth grade, you can imagine that? Every day after school, go down the gym, work out with boys twice his age. He not scared. He just go. His grandfather told him he gotta be strong, but he gotta be fast, too. So you know what that boy did? He take the heaviest plate off the barbell and he go run with em. Run around the gym, run down the street, run home, come back. Everything. Everything for come strong and come fast. He watch the old "Rocky" movie on video, he like drink egg and punch meat.

One time, he was playing with his friends up the park by the gym and one bee came sting him right on the eye, right on the eyelid part. Ho, his eye came super fat and swollen. Just had swell up in like couple seconds just like. All his friends was just laughing up and teasing him like that, and was hard cuz sore, eh, one bee sting you right on top your eye. And just like he was crying because his eye was all watery from the sting, yeah? But he wasn't crying, that boy. But all the other kids was teasing him like he was. So you know what that boy did? He found the yellow jacket nest. Was right on top the side of the gym right by one light. He took his hand and grabbed that yellow jacket nest and shoved it right in his face. And he was squeezing that thing and shaking 'em for make all the bees come out and the other boys was all yelling and screaming for make him stop and he neva. And all the bees came out and they was mad and they went all on top his face, on his neck, on his arms, in his clothes, everywhere he had bee stings. But he neva cry once. And all the other boys had go run away, all scared. He not scared, but. That boy not scared nothing.

After the mother and me had break up, was hard. She neva like me see him. I was kinda heavy into my using at the time. She took him up Mainland and I went inside and that was it. She said she like 'em be safe, but I told her nothing can hurt that boy. I remember how his face looked and I look at him now on top the TV and I cannot believe fifteen years already. Sometimes I write to him but I think so he real busy. And I kind of moving around a lot ever since I got out, so . . . But him, broken ankle and all, still going. That's him. That's how.

CURT LUM
(TRUE STORY)

I BLAMING THE LEMON CHICKEN.

Birthday party my friends' house in Kailua. I went once before I left, but that was the false one. I thought I was in the clear.

I could feel my stomach starting to huli about two minutes after I left the house. But shame go back. So I think, nah, jam 'em on the Like. Maybe I cannot make it to Kunia in time, but I can stop my father's house in Kalihi. Late already and he probably sleeping, but I get the key to the downstairs so I can get in without waking him up. I hope.

I think it was that big dip in Kahekili Highway by the H-3 on ramp. That set it off good.

First I'm pretty sure I can make it. Then I not so sure. Then, nah, make 'em. Then I thinking, ho, I gotta sacrifice my car upholstery. It's life or death. Pretty soon, the "nah, I can make it" phase is pretty much gone and it's all "I going die. I going die. I going die."

I take off the seat belt. No help.
I try sit forward on the seat. No help.
I try sit back on the seat. No help.
I try sit sideways on the seat. No help.
I catching chills so I turn on the car heater. No help.

I thinking if I should chance 'em and stop on the side of the freeway and if I get McDonald's napkins in the glove compartment or what but nah, dangerous. And if I gun it, I think so I can reach my father's house.

I felt like that story, "The Five Chinese Brothers," the one where the one Chinese brother swallowed the whole ocean and he had hard time keeping 'em in. He was sputtering. I was sputtering. I was flapping.

I reach my father's house and I don't even put my car in park before I jumping out, crawling across the grass. I get to the downstairs door and I looking for the keys in the dark and ho, where is the key! This one! No fit. This one! No fit. And then Ai-YA! Drop the keys! All out of time already. Right on the grass:

PRRRRRAAAAAAAH!

Next time I go my father's house, his neighbor tell me, "Eh, was you ah watering the yard at one o'clock in the morning?" I tell him had one spot look dry. He tell me, not now. Look nice and green.

VERNA
–
WAIPAHU'S ANSWER TO MARTHA STEWART

WHAT YOU GOTTA DO IS TAKE OUT THE WALL BY THE SIDE, knock out the post pillar thing you get in the corner, put the garbage cans by the side of the house and tell Rodney he gotta park his truck down the street by the hibiscus bush. Then you would have one nice place for make party.

I get 'em all in my head. You get the fridgerator already in the corner but no good because when you open the door, the thing all the time bang your Camry and hoo, get planny dings. I need one beer, ding. I like one soda, ding. I think we get little bit poke left, doosh.

You move the fridgerator in the middle, by where Rodney get the old car batteries all stack up, and then you go City Mill and get the Country Willow counter top. Make sure is the Country Willow and not the Country Oak cuz the Country Oak look shetty.

So you put up the Country Willow counter top and you get the ice cooler, the one Rodney tell he use fo go fish but he neva fish how long already, and you run the water hose from the papaya tree in the back all the way through the side of the house and you get wet bar. Either that or you hook up one tube to the kitchen, but then you going have to hemo that thing when you like wash dishes, and you twist the thing, your hand come sore.

If you go with the Country Willow counter top, then later on, you can go back and get the bar stools with the orange vinyl. Match nice. Just no ask for the orange. They no call that color orange. That's "Sunset." Get difference.

And no buy no damn wall paper for finish. You get this kind, No Bugs M'Lady. Stick on the back. Work good and more cheap.

I can help you do 'em you like, only thing I no can do electricals and I think so if you take out da wall, you gotta put the fuse box someplace else. I mean, I could figure 'em out, but nah, more better you spend couple dollars and hire one professional.

Whatever you do, no let Rodney do 'em. And no let him tell you he get one friend know how for do 'em cheap. I had one friend do 'em cheap for me when I wen remodel the bachroom at the restraunt. Now I get the only bachroom in Waipahu with the hand driers so low you can blow dry your choch.

But I help you. You can do 'em for cheap. Just no get the Country Oak. Look shetty.

DOREEN TAEZA
–
FORMER DISCO QUEEN

*T*HIS ONE, THIS ONE HERE. THE THING WITH YOUR AUNTY Dottie, started with this. This and the dress. I came home one time fo go out, I had bafe and whatnot, and I had go fo pull my dress out of the closet and I look, and I knew right there. Was one nice dress. All with lace from Foxmoor Casuals. And I had buy 'em special. Big money. Just by looking, I could tell already. Your Aunty Dottie had sneak inside my room. She had sneak inside my room, take my Foxmoor Casuals dress, wear 'em fo go out and then sneak 'em back on top the hanger like nothing happen. Like I wouldn't notice. But could tell already. Had her body shape all pressed into the polyester lining and the whole thing smelled like this damn Jean Naté crap she was always spraying by her dakine. As if that make difference.

So I go to her, "Why the hell you wearing my Foxmoor Casuals dress? Brand new. 'As mines, you know." And she go, "Like I would wear your clothes. I like NICE KINE clothes, not like the kind you get." And I told her, "Please, you still wearing your maroon Danskin skirt from the fifth grade." And she tell me, "It's burgundy, not maroon. See, you don't know nothing about clothes. You don't even know your colors."

So I go to her, "I not the one wear white shirt, black bra and think I match." And she tell me, "What, I had that look about six years before Selena, so no tell me I don't know fashion."

After that, was full war.

Had blue ink inside my shampoo bottle, had peroxide inside her conditioner. Had all the straps cut off my halter tops, had one black T-shirt get inside her white panty laundry, make everything grey. I was thinking I was going put Morning Breeze inside her Jean Naté. As if that make difference.

One time, she was out somewhere and she needed a ride so she called the house. I knew was her, so I had answer. I told her, "And to what is the purpose of this phone call ?" and she go, "Ho, Doreen, you talking big now ever since you got dat job answering phones at Budget Rent A Car." And I go, "Shut up, at least I have a job." And she go, "I get one job." And I told her, "Stealing quarters from the newspaper machine with one chopstick and bubble gum no count as one job." And she told me, "What, like Budget Rent A Car is all that." And I told her, "What, you stuck? You need ride? Maybe you should call Budget Rent A Car come pick you up."

So that's how come things is the way it is with me and your Aunty Dottie. And look, she work Alamo now. And that's why every year, Christmas time, I wrap up that damn Foxmoor Casuals dress and give it back to her. Birthday time, she wrap 'em up and try give 'em back to me. But I tell her, I no like 'em now. It's ruined. The whole damn thing smell like that crap Jean Naté.

Eh, that's Uncle Richard over there. Go tell him hi. But no go inside the car with him, OK? Just tell him hi.

95

TSUKEBE UNCLE RICHARD

*C*OME, BEBE,
come over here.
Come talk to uncle.
Uncle never see you long time.
Here, come more close.
Uncle's eyes no can see too good already.
I like see how big you came.
Come, bebe.
No just stand over there.

Come give uncle one kiss.
That's the way. That's how.
You big girl already, eh? Some big you coming.
What is that?
Mosquito bites?
How one mosquito got over there and over there, ha?
Ah, uncle just teasing you.
You know uncle, always joking around yeah?
Good fun, eh? That's why I your favorite.

Come over here, sweetheart.
Uncle miss you.
So long already neva see.

You rememba before time when uncle had his dirt bike?
You rememba?

Ho, uncle used to take you kids riding all the time yeah?
Was good fun,
you rememba?
Uncle used to take you and your braddah riding up cane fields all the way
by the water tank, yeah?
How much times uncle took you guys.
And then aftah, go eat Dairy Queen, yeah?
Ho, the good fun we used to have, yeah?
Uncle miss that already.
Uncle miss you.
Maybe uncle should go get dirt bike again, yeah?
Me and you go riding in the fields, go to the water tank again.
You would like that, ha, girl?
Good fun go with uncle by the water tank.
Ho, uncle would like that, I tell you.
Uncle would enjoy.

Why you standing so far over there, bebe?
Uncle not going bite you.
Just like you going more far.
Why, uncle smell good.

I get my aftahshave, 'as why.
'As musk.
Come smell over here where uncle when put.
Come.
Come smell.
Smell good.
You going like 'em. I promise.

Come sit over here.
Sit on uncle's lap.
Come, just like when you was small kid time, yeah?
Ho, uncle miss you so much I tell you.
Come sit on uncle's lap.
That's it. That's the way.
Wait, move little bit this side.

97

There you go.
There you go.

You so pretty. You coming so pretty, I tell you girl.

Where your mada?
She stay?
She came down?
Oh, over there.
She looking?
Here, ne'mind uncle's lap. Uncle get sore leg anyway.
Get off already. Get off.
Go over there, go help your mada.
That's it.
Ho, you coming so big already.
You one big girl.

BILL THOMPSON

—

NEVER USES A SHOPPING CART

I DON'T EVEN KNOW THE BOY'S NAME, BUT I KNOW HE LIKES the chocolate ones the best.

I saw him. He didn't know I was home. I did that on purpose. I wanted to see his reaction.

Coupla months back, I think I'm going crazy. I could have sworn I had leftover spaghetti in the fridge, but I get home after work and it's not there. Stuff was going missing all the time. Little stuff, like the last few cookies in a bag or I coulda sworn the orange juice carton was full and now it's almost gone. Stuff like that.

Just so happened I stayed home from work one day. Just so happened my car was in the shop. I'm lying on the couch and I hear this noise in my kitchen. The scrape of the louvers sliding on the metal clips. I think, whoa! So that's it! Some crack addict has been breaking into my house and ripping off my stuff! I grab a 9-iron out of the bag and head toward the kitchen. I'm thinkin I'll call the cops after I nail this guy myself, and that way I'm sure justice will be served. So I turn the corner to the kitchen and I've got the golf club raised over my head like I'm going to kill a bear and I see this kid. He's maybe nine or ten years old, skinny as can be, and he's sitting square in the middle of my kitchen eating the chocolate cookies out of a chocolate-vanilla two-pack. He left the vanilla alone, and he left four of the chocolate untouched. He put the package back on the counter just where I had it. He wiped his hands on his shirt and he was gone the way he came, louvers put back, cookies in their place.

99

I couldn't sleep that night. Something about his face.

Next day, I buy this big basket and fill it up with everything I could think of: candy, bread, juice boxes, chips, and those chocolate cookies. I left the basket right on the lanai, right under the louvered window to the kitchen. I put a little note on it that said "For you" and I figured he'd get it. That basket stayed there for a week. Untouched. But stuff kept going missing from my fridge. And when I looked real hard, I could see chocolate fingerprints on the louvers. I could see where he moved the basket to get to the window ledge and then put it back when he left.

I left a twenty dollar bill on the kitchen counter one time. Nothing. He left it right there but he took my leftover kung pao take-out.

So now, I keep a little extra food in the fridge. I make sure I always have those cookies. And when my landlord asked me if I was having any problems with the apartment and would I like to move to a higher floor, I told him no. I like it where I am.

KAYLA CAMPOS
—
CAN HĀPAI 20-POUND BAGS OF FRISKIES

I WAS, LIKE, SIX YEARS OLD WHEN I FOUND MY FIRST MYRTLE. She was just a small kitten living underneath the steps by the old dispensary. She was one-side makapō at first, but then her eyes opened and she could see everything. I was all by myself when I found her, and good thing, because if I was with my brothers maybe they woulda hurt her. But was just me, so I could take her and wrap her in my jacket before somebody saw and did something.

Myrtle lived in our washhouse underneath the skip that lifted up the washing machine for when the yard flooded out. That only happened in big rain, but we had big rain kinda plenty.

My dad told me she was pretty because she had a turtle shell coat and I thought that was hilarious because how can a cat have a turtle shell? Cat is cat and turtle is turtle. But then I thought, turtle, like honu, like our 'aumakua, which can change and shift and sometimes be anything. That's why I called her Myrtle. Myrtle turtle. She would protect me and I would protect her.

My mother didn't like Myrtle too much. She didn't like me sneaking milk and hamburger and vienna sausage to feed her and she didn't like Myrtle making messes, which Myrtle hardly ever did. My mom didn't just not like messes. She didn't like potential of messes. She let me keep Myrtle but only outside and only under condition of no messes.

When Myrtle got too big for under the skip, she moved herself to on top of the tool shelf in the garage and sometimes on the hood of the car, which I had to be very careful not to let my mom see. When it was cold, sometimes she liked to sleep underneath the car or in the engine.

That Myrtle went away the same night my dad left. I thought maybe my father took her with him. For protection. My mother said my father was working for the state and had to live away from us for a while. She told me Myrtle went to live with a nice coffee farmer in Kona who needed her help catching all the rats. I almost said that Myrtle doesn't eat rats, she eats vienna sausage, but then I remembered and I kept my mouth quiet.

For a long time I thought about my dad working hard for the state and missing us every every day, but he didn't write and he didn't call and him missing us was only what I imagined. Myrtle didn't come back to visit me either, but I looked all over for her. She sent me a message, though. Another turtle shell kitten that looked just like her was at the old dispensary. I called that kitten Myrtle. My number two brother told me "You cannot name a girl name like a junior!" and I told him she's not a Myrtle junior. She's just a Myrtle and I can name her whatever I want.

I told my second brother that he and nobody else better hurt Myrtle because she's watching over the whole family. He told me I didn't know what I was talking about. That my dad didn't go away for work, that he was taken away and wasn't coming back. And that there was no coffee grower in Kona who needed help for catching rats. Mommy didn't want me to know the truth.

When nobody else was around, I held Myrtle in my arms real close and I let my tears fall into her fur. I asked her what was the for real truth and she told me my Dad missed me more than he could say and that's why he doesn't say it and she told me her and all the Myrtles and turtles would watch over him and me always.

DOTTIE TAEZA-TABALNO
–
DOREEN'S SISTER

TELL HER IT'S FOR SCHOOL. TELL HER YOU NEED IT FOR A FIELD trip or something. Not a field trip. Tell her books. You gotta buy books for school. Tell her the books are kind of expensive and you're really sorry but you want to do good so you have to have the books or you're gonna be left behind. Tell her that.

No, wait. She'll write you a check. Don't do that. Tell her it's for shopping. Tell her you going to the swap meet with your friend. Don't say you're going with me. Say you're going with your friend. If she asks, tell her you going with your school friends, not your neighborhood friends. Don't tell her names because then she can check.

Tell her you need cash because they don't take check or credit card at the swap meet. I mean, if she gives you a credit card, you can take that too, but try to get the cash.

You understand, right? It's not a bad thing. It's a good thing. You're helping me out. You know you're my favorite of all the nieces and nephews. You're the only one I can trust. I would ask her myself but her and me, we don't always understand each other. Not like you and me. You and me, we're close.

Just, when you talk to her, act all casual and don't give too many details. Keep it simple. Hard to remember when you give plenty details and you don't want her to start thinking nothing.

Go talk to her now and then meet me by the bridge. I'll be right there on the side by the bushes by the water. Go now and I meet you there. And don't you mention my name, okay? Tell her you selling candy for school and you got hungry and ate 'em all and you have to pay it back. Tell her, okay? Go now and come right back.

"JOE BOY"

MY FIRST TATTOO WAS A PRESENT FROM MY MOTHER. A present on my fourteenth birthday. She wanted me to have an eagle like her boyfriend at the time. I wanted a snake with fangs curling around my arm. My friend told me Hawai'i doesn't have eagles or snakes so I should get a shark or something. I ended up with a dagger right here on my chest. See? It's like it's stabbing my heart. My mother was mad because she said she wanted me to have tattoos to make me strong, and the dagger made me weak the way it was poking into me.

I got lots of more tattoos after that. My mom stopped bugging me about the eagle after she broke up with that boyfriend, but she wanted me to have her name on my arm, so I got this when I turned eighteen. My mom liked the heart but she was mad that there was an arrow through it and blood dripping. She said my heart should be pure, but I still liked it. I got this one here by my neck and this other one on my leg. See? They're all knives. I got my sword, my dagger, and my switchblade with me at all times.

Once I started with the blades I never really thought about getting the eagle again. And then one time, me and my girlfriend was in bed and she saw the scar I have on the back, back here, and she goes, "Baby, this place here, this place where that man cut you, it looks just like a snake." So there you go.

WANDA YAMADA
–
PHARMACY GROUPIE

YOU SEE ALL THIS? STARTED WITH MY LEG.

Couple six, seven years ago, I'm sitting at the bar at Restaurant Row in my short black dress, same like every other woman sitting at the bar at Restaurant Row in a short black dress, and I doing the move with my leg and I feel this thing. Like a lump, but smaller. Like a bump, but bigger.

So I ran my hand down my leg, kinda sexy so looks like it's part of my act, and I felt it and it was kinda hard and raised and scaly. I took my French manicure nail and I started picking at this thing. But the thing didn't want to pick. I broke off my acrylic and the thing was still there.

I go home that night, look in the bathroom under the fluorescent light and the thing has one eye. One eye! I thought about making my own surgery with a tweezers and a safety pin but that thing was looking at me.

I was so scared. I started thinking that it was maybe my fetal twin, absorbed inside my body in the womb and now coming out after all these years, bone and hair and ay, Jesus, maybe get teeth inside there. I read that one time in the *National Enquirer*.

So when I sleep at night, I scared the teeth so I put one pillow in between my knees so the teeth no bite or spread or whatever. Except pillow isn't good enough protection so I gotta sleep with my legs little bit apart so it doesn't jump straight through the pillow to the other side.

That's how I jam up my hip, sleeping all like that. You jam up your hip, next thing to go is your feet. I gotta wear orthopedics.

When you get feet problems, next come the knee problems. Ace bandage. Two side. With a little hole cut on the side with the thing so that the teeth can breathe.

After the knee problems came the back problems. That's why I get the brace.

Look at me. Pau the short black dress.

And I get all this stuff going on, I cannot sleep I so worried and upset. You no sleep, you get all kind health problems. Heart, lung, kidney, spleen. I was falling apart, I tell you.

So I going doctor, one 'nother doctor, one specialist in spleenology or whatever, and he just so happen to look my leg and he says, oh, you have a wart on the inside of your leg. One wart. One wart! Here, he says, let me get that for you. Ssslp. Stitch. Gone.

So I thinking that maybe everything else going go away too. Not yet, but I hoping. And all that time, I was so sure had teeth.

OFFICER WOLVERTON KAHAUNAELE

*T*HE SUSPECT WAS FIRST OBSERVED BY ME GOING EASTBOUND on the westbound lane in a northwesterly direction. The suspect vehicle was determined to be a 1983 El Camino, blue and primer yellow, license plate KEG 298. The vehicle in question was weaving in and out of traffic and in the process hit two parked cars, a pedestrian, sixteen traffic cones, a City and County median sprinkler head, and a chicken. The City and County Department of Sprinkler Maintenance was immediately notified. While in pursuit of the rogue vehicle, I did not turn on my DIV (Department Issued Vehicle) lights and sirens because I didn't want to scare nobody and besides, on H-1 during rush hour, nobody can get out of the way even if they try. Maximum speed during said pursuit did not exceed maximum speed mandated minimum as referred to in SHOPO collective bargaining agreement section 23-14-45 A, subsection 2-Z under the heading "whippas."

It was determined by me that the vehicle in question was that of a stolen vehicle determined by the number of so-called dings around the door handles, the bumper sticker reading "My child is an honor student," which seemed not to match the appearance and demeanor of the suspect, and the fact that the driver did not seem to know where the controls for the turn indicator and windshield wipers were located. I determined this through the process of observation, and by the elderly female in the back of the car who appeared to be tied up with a binding material of some sort with the appearance of chintz. Upon closer observation by me and by a subsequent arresting officer, the woman had indeed been bound, but the binding material in question appeared to be that of apparent manapua wrappers that had been glued together with tape.

After the suspect vehicle came to rest in the fountain at Honolulu Hale, I and Officer Barrington Magarifuji arrived at the scene and assessed the danger to said parties and other parties that were in the neighboring vicinity and surrounding areas of which there were none. At this time, we approached the vicinity of the El Camino which was filling with water at a rate that could be classified as rapid. Officer Magarifuji approached the rear of the vehicle to assess the condition of the before-mentioned elderly female tied up with the manapua paper. It was at this time that the suspect emerged from the driver's side window of the vehicle and spoke to us in a garbled but threatening manner. Assessing the situation and referring to the SHOPO revised standards manual handbook of regulatory procedures, it was at this time that I determined to draw my gun and fire a shot in the direction of the suspect who was, in my determination, a threat to life and property, of which included the before mentioned City and County fountain. It was at this time that the Mayor was grazed, but due to the nature of the before-mentioned circumstances and the vicinity of the sprays of water from the fountain that were shooting and spraying, it is undetermined at this time where the bullet in question originated at this time.

JOHN "JOHNNY" "JOHN-BOY" MONROVIA

So I SAYS TO HIM, THIS IS HOW I GO, I GO: YOUR HONOR, I come before you to throw my mercy on this court right here to plead to you my pleadings of the facts of this case. To tell you the truth, Judge, I look at the charges my ex had allegeded against me and I'm dumbfound. This thing she get right here about how I had grab da torch welder and go for melt da ring on top her finger, das all outta porportionated right there. I never did threaten my ex with violences. In fact, I never was in possessions of one torch welder, and the torch welder I had before was stolen way before the event of the incident in question of which I facing charges.

The thing is, Your Honor, I am not a violent man. Look at my record. That speaks for himself right there. What, petty larceny, theft two, extortion. Nothing. I never been convicted of no violent crimes, and all the assault stuff on there, that's all misdemeanors back from when I was coaching Little League.

In fact, Judge, to tell you the honest truth, it is me who is really the one got perpetrated on of victimization. It's hard to admit, but I am an abused man. Das right. I not proud, but I say it right here so dat maybe odda mans can hear my story and know that they not alone. My wahine gave me dirty lickens. Planny. All the time. Ho, she used to beef me up, black eye, broken nose, everything. Look my nose. Can see the fracturcation, yeah? Das from her. And me, I man eh. I no fight back. I just take it like mans is suppose to take it. She come at me full barrel with the, the, the, the, what you call that now? The hair dryer. No! The iron curler. No, what is that? The waffle maker. That's it. She come at me full barrel with the waffle maker, all waffle

110

batter all over all stuck whatnot and she just blast me. Poom! Right there. That's assault and batter. Little bit more manslaughter was. I not lying, Judge. That's what I had to live through. Das what I had to endures.

So actually, Judge, what I saying is I should be getting one temporarily restrainment order against her cuz she da violent one. She dangerous, I tell you. Specially when she get hers. Hoo! I fear my life. I really do.

But den she go make all these trump up charges against me. Try make reverse psychologies. How can? I am not a violent man, Your Honor. I am a respect member of the community. I little more get my GED. And I'm a father. That's right, my baby girl just was born two, three months ago. Her name is Tejia-Ann or something like that. Deja, Tejia, the mother told me but I forget. These allegeded charges of which are all false I neva do, Your Honor. I promise. I neva have one torch welder long time.

Pretty good, eh? I get the lawyer talk down.

"KAHUNA DAVE"

*I*F YOU'RE LOOKING FOR THE ULTIMATE EXPERIENCE IN relaxation and harmony in your Hawaiian vacation, look no further.

The ancient Hawaiians knew the secret to health, longevity, and pace.
They turned to the ocean and to what they referred to as the "physicians of the sea"—the dolphins.
Hawaiians would swim out to the ocean and call to their dolphin friends:
"A hana laka laka zulu!"
whenever they were feeling tired or sick or stressed or whatever.
And the dolphins would hear them and come.

Through their amazing sonar techniques, which of course have inspired many of modern medicine's latest breakthroughs in healing, the dolphins know just what is wrong and just how to help.

And you can experience this ancient Hawaiian miracle of dolphin-healing, too.
And the best part—it's all free. Totally free.
The ancient Hawaiians believed you can't put a price on health and we believe that, too.
We do ask a small donation of $185 per person to help support the work of our non-profit foundation,
Dolphin Aloha.

What we'll do is take you and all members of your party to a secret, private beach.

We'll pick you up from your hotel in our foundation's Dolphinmobile for a small fee on top of the donation.
Then we'll take you to a totally private beach, teach you the ancient Hawaiian dolphin call, and lead you into the water where the physicians of the sea will come to you and heal you of your specific ailment, which they will be able to diagnose.

Sometimes they will heal you by bumping or brushing up against you.
Sometimes they might splash nearby.
Other times, the dolphins sense that the best thing is to swim about 400 yards away from you and just send you long distance sonar. When they do this, you might not even see them, but you will feel something happening and that's the most powerful form of dolphin healing of all.

After this, we'll take you back to your hotel and if you're so moved, you can make an additional donation to our cause, as many people are moved to do to express their gratitude to the dolphins.
Because really,
it's all about taking care of them.

Today is a little stormy so you probably don't want to stay by the hotel pool all day.
The private dolphin beach where we'll take you is always sunny because the dolphins make sure of it.
They want you to come. They love helping people. They're waiting for you right now.
Don't let them down.
They're dolphins.

HARRIET YAMASAKI

–

RETIRED FROM THE CREDIT UNION

*I*FINALLY DID GET RID OF THAT, WHAT YOU CALL? TELEPHONE salesperson. Telemarketer.

I read about how to do that in the magazine at my doctor's office. I go doctor plenty so I get plenty time to read all what he get inside the waiting room.

But this story wasn't about how to get rid of the kind telemarketer. Was one story story, like for entertainment. Like spooky kind. Was about this wahine on the Mainland in one of those kind places where get beach but it's cold. East Coast kind place. And she all the time, all the time get this crazy man call her on her telephone, say any kind stuff, breathe, scare her like that. She was so scared she couldn't even stand for the phone to ring. Me, I was getting little bit that way, too. The phone ring, me, I jump. But I didn't have the kind scary kind crazy man. Me, I had the telemarketer.

So this lady in the story, the one she live by the cold beach, she get this idea one day that when the crazy man call her up, she going give it right back to him the same way except she going give back more. Be more crazy. So that's what she did. She told him all the kind things like to insult him and make him feel shame for calling her. She told him like he was weak and pupule and how shame that all he get for do in his life is call people he don't even know and make trouble to get his jollies. And she told him like if she was him, she no could live with herself and would be so shame that she would take a gun and shoot herself dead from the shame. And this lady, only one time she did this, but she did it so good, she made her words come out so good and so strong, she hear one BANG on the other end of the phone and come to find out that the crazy guy did kill himself because of all what the lady was saying to him.

I read that, I think wow. That's one strong lady can talk one crazy guy into doing that kind stuff. But then I didn't think nothing. I mean, I didn't think nothing about me like that. But the thing must have stuck in my head.

Couple weeks later, I getting ready to go to my doctor appointment and my phone ring and ring. I thinking must be my doctor saying if I can come later or maybe that's my daughter telling me she cannot leave work to pick me up. So I coming fast fast out of the bathroom to answer the phone and I little bit more fall down and break my leg. I didn't fall down, but almost.

I answer the phone and it's the guy. Not the same guy, the telemarketer, but from the same place and I think so this one did call me one time before. And I was mad because I was rushing, rushing, and little bit more fall down because of him. But then he was talking to me and using my first name and that was what made me think of the story in the magazine about the lady on the cold beach. The crazy man would use her first name. I think that was special to make her more scared. For me, that just made me mad.

So I say to the man, the telemarketer, I say, "You know my first name so you must know a lot about me, yeah?" And he says, "Excuse me?" and I say, "No, I don't think I will." And I say 'em sassy and . . . kinda feel good. So I keep going. I say to him, "You must know my first name, my last name, my middle name, my maiden name. You must know where I live and how long I live here. You must have all that on your computer right in front your face. Must be because you call me up every day try sell me something. Maybe you know that one time I said yes and all that money, eighty dollars, gone and my daughter was so mad with me. Must be you put that on your computer and on the part where it asks if I'm a sucker, yes or no, you must have put yes. Well, I want you to put something else on your computer. I want you to put that this lady is crazy. Pupule. Out of her mind. Put that you call her up and she yell at you and tell you she going kick you in the 'ōkole and poke out your eye and broke your nose. Put down that I used dirty cuss words when you call me up. Put down on your computer that I called you asshole, because I just did. Put down that I told you your mother must be so shame her boy can only get this kind low-pay job calling up strangers and bothering them and trying to sell them things they don't want. Shame for your mother. Shame for your family. If I was you, I would get one gun and shoot myself dead. Asshole!"

Well, after I said that I was expecting to hear BANG. But all I heard was the click. The telemarketer don't call anymore. But sometimes I wish he would. That was good fun.

VIOLA PEROS

—

NAIL SCULPTOR

MY NEIGHBOR, SHE COME MY HOUSE AND SHE ASK ME babysit her Squeaky while she on a trip. I go "Vegas again?" because she always ask me watch the dog when she go Vegas. But she goes, "No I'm going to Colombia to have my eyes done." Well, I never did hear of this so I'm thinking is Colombia in a state or what? But her face was all serious. That's when I figured out Colombia was a country, and not the kind of country like Paris or London. The dangerous kind.

I tell her why you gotta go so far for make surgery? Get pretty good doctors right here in Liliha. She tell me no, they don't do that kind surgery in America. Only Colombia. I tell her, that don't tell you that maybe the thing little bit, oh I don't know, DANGEROUS?! She tell me no worry. Not too many tourist murders or hostage situations there lately so just take care the dog, water the plants, and bring the mail in the house if I no mind. I tell her I no mind. Cute the dog Squeaky. And small so if he make trouble on my leg, I can just fly 'em with one good shake.

Then, she tell me about the box. She go, "If something should happen to me, there's something I need you to do." And I'm like, oh, of course. No worry. We friends long time, ever since me and my first ex bought the house how long ago. And I'm thinking she going tell me I gotta take Squeaky if she die or something. But no, she goes, "There's a box underneath my bed. If something should happen to me, I need you to take that box and throw the whole thing away." Ho! Me, I thinking, why, you get somebody's head inside there or what? Because you know, I love my

CourtTV. She tell me, "Never mind what's in the box. You don't need to know what is in the box. Just do as I say and don't ask questions."

Wow.

So of course, she was gone from her house five minutes before I was in there and hunting for that thing.

Was under her bed. All wrapped with choke tape. Too small to be a head and the thing made noise when you shake 'em. Had plenty stuff inside. Ho, I wanted to look but had so much tape, no ways I could wrap 'em back like nothing if I took all that off. I put 'em back and walked the dog, but the whole time, I was thinking about that box.

Ten days she was gone and every day I was thinking how the hell am I going to look inside that damn box. I figured I knew what she had inside. I mean, I didn't think she was that kind wahine, but you never know a freak by the cover. But still, I wanted to check that thing out. I thought of all kind ways, like slit 'em on the side or buy one nodda same-kind box. One day, I no could take it. I was tired planning already. Cannot unwrap one box like that without somebody figuring out what you had do. Just like Christmas when your parents bust you for peeking inside your presents. Can always tell. So I just had bust 'em open. Ripped that bugga up. I no care she know what I did.

You know what she had inside? Three plastic cups, four batteries and a note that said, "Squeaky never liked you."

Yeah, so I don't know who taking care of that stupid rat dog now, but it ain't me. See? Those kind twisted people with the dirty mind. You never know.

GINNY DIAS

–

STILL HAS TO GO DRY CLEANERS, BANK, AND GAS STATION

*P*EANUT BUTTER, GLAD BAGS, TAMPAX, SOAP.
Peanut butter, Glad bags, Tampax, soap.
Peanut butter, Glad bags, Tampax, soap.
Peanut butter, Glad bags, Tampax. Oh, yeah, Advil.
Peanut butter, Glad bags, Advil, soap . . . uh . . .
Tampax, Glad bags, peanut butter, soap?
Oh! Miller Lite, Advil, Tampax, soap.
Wait now, Miller Lite, Tampax, dental floss?
No. Colgate? Wait. Peanut butter, Tampax, Miller Lite . . . .
Uh. OK. Peanut butter, Tampax, Glad bags, toothpick,
Downy fresh spring, nail polish remover, coffee filters,
AHHHHHHH! Ne'mind already.

V.

MR. AND MRS. LONGS

GEORGIE KAM
–
OFTEN DOESN'T BUY ANYTHING

I HAD THIS DREAM.

It wasn't like a dream dream like when you sleeping. More like the kind dream when you not sleeping, just laying in bed next to your good-for-nothing husband listening to him fut and snore. Fut. Snore. Fut. Snore. Like anybody could sleep through that noise and that stink.

So I lying there not really daydreaming cuz it's night, but not dreaming dreaming because I cannot sleep in that frickin Iraqi war zone fut snore fut snore coming in like bombs.

In this dream, I'm Mrs. Longs.

I'm the same me, but I'm married to the man, Mr. Longs. Not the brother or one of the sons, mind you. The first one, the first Mr. Longs.

We live upstairs in one of the Longses, up above the pharmacy, where we can look out the glass windows at all the shoppers when we walking from the living room to the kitchen. Hello, little shoppers! Are all you happy shoppers happy today? Oh look, sweetheart—that's what I call Mr. Longs, I call him sweetheart when we in our upstairs above the pharmacy house, but never when we in the store. When we in the store I call him Mr. Longs just like all his employees. But at home when we looking out the glass at all our aisles and all our shoppers, I tell him sweetheart, look at all our Longsness.

And I would be happy.

I would never leave the house. No need. Only time I go out now is to go Longs. I would have everything right there. Go right downstairs for cereal. Go right downstairs for shampoo. Go right downstairs when I need coffee. But I would always get dressed first. I would never go downstairs in nightgown and curlers. And I would always pay. The real kind pay, with money through the check-out line, not sign one paper and walk out the back. Mr. Longs wouldn't like that, and me, I like keep Mr. Longs happy.

I treat Longs with respect. I know that Longs isn't mine. It doesn't belong to only me. Not even to Mr. Longs. Longs is for everyone.

And if ever had hurricane or flood or whatnot, I would help Mr. Longs with whatever he need.

We would bring all our employees and all our customers inside the store, let them have anything they like, take them upstairs to our upstairs Longs house and give them tuna sandwich and tell them everything is gonna be alright don't worry don't worry. We always have Longs. Longs will provide.

Longs would be like the richest kingdom and Mr. Longs is the wise, noble king, and me, I would be the queen.

The good queen of Longs.

And I dream and I dream about my life in Longs until one extra loud snore or fut wake me up all the way and I think, ah, well. At least I know I can visit Longs tomorrow. Gotta go get Gas-X and breathing strips for him. Nose clip and ear plugs for me.

GRAMPA JOJI
–
STILL WEARS PLANTATION KHAKIS

*B*EFORE TIME NOT LIKE NOW.

We had pride back then.

We work hard.

When come night time, we go sleep. We was tired.
No go out drink, no go out cruise the town, no go out dance with any kind
wahines, no dress up like one six-foot-three Liza Minelli like your cousin
Bobby and walk around downtown scaring the homeless people.

We went sleep. We was tired.

We word hard 'as why.

Hard time work plantation.
But we neva have choice, you see.
Only had plantation.
Only job was hard labor.
You folks nowadays with your e-mail and whatnot. You no understand
what is work.
You think so one hard job is the kind your boss no let you wear nose ring
to work.
You don't know what is hard.

Hard is when you bend over hoe hana so long that when you pau work, no can stand up straight anymore.

Hard work is when get one centipede in your boots and he biting, biting all the way up your leg but you cannot stop to hemo pants. That is hard work.

Hard work is when the sickle stuck to your hand from all the blood that came out and dried up and you gotta wash your hand in the ditch water fo' letta go.

That is hard work.

You sleep good after that.
Your kaukau taste mo good.
Your coffee get good flavah.

HARVEY CARVALHO

—

GROUP LEADER

YOU KNOW YOU AIN'T LIVING YOUR LIFE RIGHT IF YOU ashamed to be seen in Longs.

If you walking down an aisle and you see somebody you know and you fast like duck over to the side aisle before they make eye contact, then you know. You got some atonement you gotta make. You got some amends in arrears.

Me, that's my test.

That's how I know.

I been on my spiritual path for fourteen years now.

Clean and sober.

Clean and mostly sober.

Never did have that awareness that they say you get after walking the path a while. Never did have those alarms that go off. Recognize the triggers. So I go to Longs, man. I go when it's busy and I walk up and down those aisles and I make it my test.

And I was doing good, I was doing real good. Months of walking in Longs with my head held high, my eyes up, back tall.

And then I saw this girl. Oooh. I forgot about her.

I wouldn't call it a full-on slip, but I couldn't look at her.

I ducked.

I ducked, man, right into the next aisle, down the side, out the door.

I went home and, man, I cried. I cried because I knew . . . I wasn't there yet.

LARRY TANOUYE
—
LONGS STOCK CLERK

SOME OF THIS STUFF, SHET, I DON'T EVEN KNOW WHAT IS this. You gotta buy this kind stuff, you in bad shape, you know what I'm saying.

Ah, like I get room for talk. What I need, dis place no sell.

If I only had a brain,
a heart,
da nerve.

Shet.

Sixteen years old, still in high school, world is my clam chowder and I figure, eh, get one job summer time, make some cash, fix up my car. So I come work over here. Rip boxes, stock shelves, take break. At least it's not "Would you like to super size that?"

My friends come inside the store, hoo, fast I dig back to the storeroom.

Not like I shame, but shet, shame!

So one day, one of the workers, Nadine, she buss me running away from my friends inside the store. She catch me in the back part by the break room and she tell me, what? Why you hiding over here? You shame? You shame your friends see you? Why you shame for?
And I tell her nah, because this ain't me.

And she go, who you then?

And I told her I not going work here the rest of my life. I going college. I taking Japanese AND Spanish. I going into international business. I going own my own company, my own jet, travel the world. This is just a summer thing. I not going be here long time. I get plans.

And she tell me yeah, that's what we all said.

That was thirteen years ago.

She was right.

Bitch.

And the real pisser is she still stay, too, and every day I come in, she tell me, "So Larry, how's those plans?"

Maybe some of this stuff would help because, damn, I am stuck.

JOSEPHINE LEI PERALTA

—

WAITING TO CATCH BUS

HOW COME ALL YOU YOUNG KIDS THINK OLD PEOPLE IS smart? Like you think when you past sixty-five you collect Social Security checks and you collect brains, too. Like some kind wisdom you never had your whole life jess kick in. That's baloney. No treat old folks like we know more just cause we older than you. We not smart. We just old.

Look at me. I'm seventy-three years old and I'm stupid. I'm more stupid today than I was forty years ago.

I been married five times, and every one was more worse than the one before. I quit drinking and smoking forty years ago and my life was downhill ever since. Now the doctor says I going die of skin cancer. Shit, I could have been enjoying my whiskey and my cigarettes all this time. Wouldn't have made difference.

You come to me and go, "Grandma, I so confused. I don't know what to do. Please help me." And I like tell you, "Damn kid, hell if I know. If I was you, I would go out, buy one pack cigarettes, get drunk, and no worry. You young yet. What the hell?"

Your cousin came my house last week and told me, "Grandma, I like do this but I think maybe so I should do that. What would da old Hawaiians do?" I told him, "Da fuck if I know!" Yeah, I old and yeah, I Hawaiian, but when I was growing up, I neva work taro patch. I worked pineapple cannery. But you don't understand, yeah? Old is old to you. Old is wise.

I tell you, good you get respect for your elders and all that, but no make me one fucking leader of your tribe. I neva did nothing special my whole life. I got married, I had kids, I watched TV. That's it. My kids not even special, and your Uncle Tommy got arrested two times.

So you gotta go find one nodda old lady for be your kupuna because I lived long time but I neva figure out shit.

CORY CHOW
—
TOO BIG TO RIDE IN THE SHOPPING CART BUT CAN POP WHEELIES WITH 'EM

ME AND MY TWO COUSINS TOOK NOTICE THAT ALL OUR grampa's drink-beer-in-the-garage friends got these cool nicknames. There's Legs, Fingers, Blackie, Whitey, Sexy, Menpachi—who they call Pachi—and our grandfather, who they call Uku. We don't know why they call him Uku, but must be something from when they were small.

Me and my two cousins, we're not allowed to ask about the nicknames. We're not allowed to call any of them by the nicknames. We're not supposed to even say them out loud. We tried one time, little bit sly, like, "Ho, Uncle Pachi, can pass the poke?" And our grandfather gave us the mean dirty look and that was it. We never did it again. I mean, to ourselves, when we climbed up on the roof and listened to them in the garage, we would say stuff like, "Fingers in the sauce again" or "You can call me Sexy" and we would crack up, but soft so they wouldn't hear.

Who would think three punk kids would look up to a bunch of old men? But they were cool. They were tough. They had their own gang. They knew stuff and kept secrets. They could spot a scam, they could hold their liquor, they could make you believe the most unbelievable lie.

Me and my two cousins came up with our own nicknames. My one cousin was Prince, my other cousin was Duke, and I was King. Terrible. So we changed. My one cousin was Lefty, my other cousin was Lucky, and I was Lexus. So stupid because Lefty wasn't a lefty, Lucky wasn't lucky, and I didn't even have a bike let alone a car. Try again. My one cousin is Ace, my other cousin is Deuce, and I'm Trey. After a while we figured out it doesn't work that way. You can't just pick out your cool nickname. Something cool has to happen or your friends tease you about something and that's how you get the name. But nothing cool ever happened and the only tease names we had were Fut, Futhead, and Futboy.

One time me and my two cousins were sleeping over my grandfather's house. I fell asleep on the couch watching TV but my two cousins went sleep inside the bedroom. My grandfather came in from the garage and saw me sleeping there so he woke me up to go inside sleep in the bedroom. But when he woke me up, he said, "Bones. Bones. Go sleep in the bedroom." I woke up all the way and sat up on the couch, all excited. "Is that my nickname?" "Your what?" "Did you just give me my nickname?" My grandfather told me, "No, I just forgot your name and you the skinny one compared to your fat cousins."

But my grandfather, he was so good, he knew why I was asking. And every time after that, when was just me at his house without my two cousins, he called me "Bones," and sometimes, even in the garage in front of all of his friends.

ALFRED PINTO
—
CITY AND COUNTY PENSION

*L*OOK ALL WHAT THEY BEEN PUT OVER HERE. LOOK ALL
the buildings and whatnot. Cannot see the ocean. How you supposed to
know you live Hawai'i if cannot see the ocean? And how close the ocean.
Just right over there. Boop! But cannot see with all what they been put.

Look over there. How the hell, you tell me. You think so they got this
zoning? For put something this big? I don't think so. Must be somebody
know somebody kind of thing. Must be ho'omalimali I scratch your
back you scratch mine kind of thing. You think so if was somebody like
me I could put this kind buildings all over here? No ways. You gotta be
connected, you see. Friends in high places is what it is.

I was living over here fifty years. Fifty years! Never did make no trouble to
nobody. When they wanted to put up all the buildings, the man, he came.
Two guys. They came my house talk to me, try get me sign, try give me
money. But only little bit. I tell them, that's not what this house is worth.
They try offer me little bit more. I tell them no, that's not the point. What
is money? This is my home, you see. My home where I can look the ocean
right over there. Night time I can look the moon through the coconut
trees and see all the kind stars because dark the sky, no more lights from
no buildings.

But now, look. No more stars. Get all the lights they been put on all the
kind buildings now they get. Me, I held on to my house. For what? Not the
same.

But I get all the palapala, you know. I save all that. All the papers I get. That's why they come all the time, they watch me, you know. They try get inside my house to get the papers. That's why I don't leave, you see. Because I get all the kind documents, and he show. He show 'em all. Not supposed to put all what they wen put all over here. I get all the papers that show. How the hell?

MARLENE KAHIKINA

—

TAKES HER AUNTIES SHOPPING

WASN'T SO MUCH THE MONEY THAT WAS MAKING ME nuts, 'kay? Was the names. Everywhere. On little pieces of tape. Under the picture. Under the lamp. Under the television. My grammada wasn't even sick yet and they all kapu-ing what they like after she dead. My grammada was little bit forgetful that time already, but she knew what they was doing, 'kay? She just didn't say nothing.

I go over her house, make coffee, OH! Get my cousin's name underneath the coffee pot. I mean, I can see the thing old and probably from the plantation days, but come on. She still using 'em. I made coffee for my grammada and that piece tape on the bottom burned off right there on the stove.

I grab the blue vase to put her favorite anthuriums inside, get my other cousin's name on one piece tape.

I went little bit nuts. I looked under everything. Made me one list. Looked again one more time. Come more mad. I asked my grammada what you know about this and she tell me better pick out what you like now because those vultures not letting you take the lint from the bottom of the drawer when I'm gone. I told her Gramma, what I like from you is you. I like you tell me all kind stories from your old plantation days. I like spend time with you. She tell me, "You sure you don't want the candy dish? It's real crystal."

When my grammada went into the hospital, I was the first one at her house. I made sure. I beat all of 'em. But I didn't take nothing. No ways, 'kay? I took all their names on those pieces tape and I had switch 'em all around. Took my one cousin's name off the vase and put 'em behind the picture. Took my other cousin's name from behind the picture and put 'em under the lamp. Like that, all through the house.

After the funeral, we had the reception at my grammada's house. All my cousins were going nuts, 'kay? Was full chaos. Me and my grammada, we was just laughing.

NADINE TAM SING
—
LONGS WORKER

END OF MY SHIFT, I CASH OUT MY REGISTER, TAKE MY drawer and I'm heading to the back office, and then I see something out of the corner of my eye. There's this lady, all dressed up, nice dress, pantyhose, black pumps, and she's like, walking on her knees down the center aisle.

I thought to myself, well, there's something I never seen before. But then, I remembered.

When I was small, I was with my mother-dem in church. We were sitting down waiting for mass to start. All of a sudden, this lady comes crawling down the aisle. Not really crawling because it wasn't hands and knees. Just knees. She was all dressed up with nylons and heels and that little scarf pinned on her head and her hands were like she was praying and she was crawling—knee crawling down the center aisle to the altar. And she was crying and crying and crying. My mom tells me don't look, don't look. And all I could think of was, what could make somebody cry like that?

And here's this lady now in the middle of the store and she's crying and crying and crying. And I'm thinking don't look, don't look.

But this is Longs. I'm Longs. She needs something.
So I go up to her and say, "Is there something you were looking for?"
And she stops dead in her knee tracks. I'm thinking maybe she lost her car keys or she's sick and she can't find the diarrhea medicine or I don't know

what. And she looks up at me and her eyes are like, I don't know, like maybe she didn't see me standing there. So I go, "Can I help you?"

Right there, she stops crying. It was like turning off a faucet. And she gets up off the floor. She looks at me, not smiling, but something . . . I don't know . . . peaceful. And she walks out of the store like nothing. That was it. I noticed the toes of her shoes left black marks all down the center aisle from 1-A to 7-B. So I locked up my cash drawer and I got the mop.

Hi, did you find everything you needed today?

Lee Cataluna was born on Maui and raised in plantation houses in Wailuku, Kōloa and Ka'u. She graduated magna cum laude from the University of the Pacific in Stockton, California in 1988, and in 1999, was awarded the honor of Distinguished Young Alumna of the University. After working ten years in local television and radio, she became a columnist for *The Honolulu Advertiser* in 2000. She has studied playwriting with Victoria Nalani Kneubuhl, Y York, and at the David Henry Hwang Playwriting Institute at the East West Players in Los Angeles. She is a 2004 winner of the Cades Award for Literature for her body of work, and served as the 2004–2005 Keables Chair at Iolani School. Her favorite stories, fiction and non-fiction, are about ordinary people struggling to live lives of dignity and purpose.

WORK INCLUDES:

Da Mayah—first produced by Kumu Kahua Theatre, September 1998; remount summer 1999; broke box office records for the theater. Subsequent productions at Maui Onstage at the Iao Theatre, January 1999, remount in 2000; University of Hawai'i-Hilo Theatre department, October 2000. Published in *He Leo Hou: A New Voice—Hawaiian Playwrights*, Bamboo Ridge Press 2003.

Ulua: The Musical—with music composed by Sean T.C. O'Malley—Kumu Kahua Theatre/McKinley High School drama department, November 1999.

Aloha Friday—winner of the Kumu Kahua/UH Drama Department Playwriting Contest Hawaii Award. Produced by Kumu Kahua Theatre, September 2000; remount summer 2001. Produced by the UH-Hilo Theatre department, November 2004.

Musubi Man—an adaptation of the book by Sandi Takayama, commissioned by Honolulu Theatre for Youth, produced spring 2002; remount with Honolulu Theatre for Youth, spring 2005.

Super Secret Squad—commissioned by Kumu Kahua Theatre, produced spring 2002.

You Somebody—with music composed by Keola Beamer. Commissioned by Diamond Head Theatre, produced summer 2002. Po'okela winner for original script. Produced by the Volcano Arts Center, August 2004.

Folks You Meet in Longs—produced by Kumu Kahua Theatre, August 2003, remounted summer 2004; toured to Maui Arts and Cultural Center, September 2004.

Kona Town Musicians—commissioned adaptation of the book by Pat Hall for Honolulu Theatre for Youth, September 2004, with neighbor islands school tour.

Half Dozen Long Stem—Kumu Kahua Theatre, October 2004.